NEANDERTHAL

2

Little Mary Ann

by

Vernon Gillen

All of Vernon's novels and books are available at Amazon.com

ISBN - #

978 - 1724414885

To The Reader

After reading some of my novels people ask if I really am a Christian. Yes I am. However; most people on this Earth are not and they use foul language when they talk. In other words the language used in my novels has a lot to be desired if you are a Christian but, it is realistic.

In all of my novels I try to be as realistic as possible. Therefore; some of the characters in my novels use foul language. I apologize for this but it is only a part of my trying to be realistic. I hope that you can overlook these "Imperfections" and still enjoy my novels.

The main characters in all of my novels are or soon become Christians and at times pray asking for God's help in something.

Vernon Gillen

Contents

Chapter 1

Game Cameras

Nine years ago Michael was captured by the government and heavily sedated before he could resist. Now he remains heavily sedated at the government underground holding facility in Northern Oklahoma. The government keeps him sedated because they feared him much more than the others that were being held there.

Evie and their daughter Mary Ann had been on the run ever since Evie had Michael's book on his experiences as the beast published. Colonel Briks and his new wife Sandy helped them. The four had become close as Briks and Sandy watched Mary Ann grow.

There was a new threat which also kept the police and military busy. Over the years terrorist have come into the country through the southern border. The first thing that a newly elected Socialist president did was bulldoze parts of the wall down that the previous two presidents had put up.

For sixteen years the nation got safer as the southern wall went up. Within two months of a Socialist moving into the White House terrorist actions against American citizens more than quadrupled. California being a Sanctuary State actually allowed terrorist training camps to be built and operated in the state.

Other liberal groups that hated the police and military started killing police and any military person off duty. Good citizens without CHL's were carrying firearms against the wishes of the police in order to protect themselves. Everyone talked about a possible Civil War.

Briks and Sandy had moved Evie and Mary Ann all over the country through the years but they were presently in east Texas. This last move was hopefully their last move. The only way to protect Mary Ann was to educate her at home but, Evie was great at that. But then one day Mary Ann showed a hint that she might have some of her father's abilities.

Mary Ann was playing in the back yard on the swing when she got to high and the swing flipped over. She was not badly hurt but she still got mad. Evie and Sandy noticed that when Mary Ann raised her hand the fallen swing slid away from her a few inches. It was not much but it was enough that the two women saw it. Evie ran outside and grabbed her daughter and ran back inside. There was no way of knowing if someone was watching.

"What's wrong Mommy?" Mary Ann asked as soon as they were back inside the home.

"How long have you been able to move things by just thinking about it?" Evie asked her daughter.

"What do you mean Mommy?" Mary Ann asked.

"You're not in trouble Baby … but I saw you move the swing." Evie said. "How did you do it?"

"It hurt me Mommy." Mary Ann replied. "It hurt me."

"I know Baby but …" Evie tried to find out how her daughter did it. "You didn't touch it and yet you made it move. How did you do that?"

"Oh … I see what you mean." Mary Ann answered. "I just thought about pushing it away and it moved away."

Evie and Sandy had a long talk with Mary Ann about her father and her newly discovered abilities. By time they finished Mary Ann understood that she could not use her abilities in front of anyone. More importantly she understood why she could not do it. She had never been told where her father was nor why but now she knew.

Evie and Sandy sat on the couch taking a few sighs of relief. Mary Ann walked over and sat in her mom's lap as if nothing had happened. As she played with her doll Evie and Sandy looked at each other. They knew that everything had changed. Mary Ann would grow up not knowing what having a friend was like. From then on they had to keep her away from anyone until she was a little older. The had to make sure that she understood the importance of not showing her abilities to anyone. Right now she was just to young to completely understand.

Mary Ann understood better than her mom thought. It had a great deal to do with the alien DNA that was injected into her father. She was more mature than other children around her. Some of the traits or abilities in her from the DNAs given to her father never showed up in her father. But things were about to change as Mary Ann discovered more abilities that she had.

None of those around Mary Ann knew why these abilities were just now showing up in her. Maybe it had to do with puberty. Maybe her body was just starting to change to the point that it started excepting the things that her DNA had in store for her.

Mary Ann had become a loner, being quiet all of the time. Looking in her eyes one could see that she was always thinking. She was almost a spooky young lady but her mother still loved her.

One day Evie, Sandy, and Mary Ann went into town to get a few groceries. As they walked into the store two cars barely bumped each other. A young man got out of one care and walked over to the other car. He opened the door to the other car and pulled out a stunned old man.

"Are you crazy old man?" the young man yelled as he shook the old man. "Look what you did to my car."

There was only a tiny scratch on the young man's car and he was the one that drove to close to the old man. The old man was in shock and said nothing.

"No!" Mary Ann said so low that Evie barely heard her.

"What Baby?" Evie asked as she looked down at her. Then she saw a change in her daughter's face that she had not seen for three years.

Suddenly Mary Ann changed as her mother and Sandy were pushed away by an unseen force. "No!" Mary Ann said again.

Suddenly the ground began to shake. A light pole leaned

over but did not fall to the ground. No one in the parking lot could stand easily. The young man crawled back to his car which began to smoke. Mary Ann took two steps forward but she was not Mary Ann anymore. She had fully changed into a teenage Neanderthal. Suddenly the ground opened under the young man's car and impartially fell into the crack.

"Don't kill him Baby." Evie begged. "Do like your father did. Just scare him."

Like when her father was the beast she could not speak but she still knew what was going on. Evie reached out and grabbed her daughter's arm. Ghe shield was no longer there. Evie, Mary Ann, and sandy went back to the pick-up and got in. Then they left and went back home.

After Sandy and Dan Briks got married he trained her to protect Evie and Mary Ann. She had become a part of God's Soldiers but did not go on missions with the others. She had one job and loved watching over Evie and her daughter.

As Evie drove home Sandy talked with Mary Ann. "You have got to learn to control this." she told Mary Ann. "What else can you do?"

"I don't know." Mary Ann told Sandy. "I didn't know I could do that."

"We need to find out what all she can do." Sandy suggested.

Evie agreed with Sandy. Once home Mary Ann would need to stay there a while as they learned more about what she could do. Hopefully no one saw Mary Ann as a Neanderthal child. Unfortunately; one person did.

As the fight started a woman started recording it on her cell phone. When Mary Ann took those two steps forward the woman saw her and turned her phone to record her. When the ground cracked and started to swallow the young man's car she turned her phone back to record that. When she looked back at Mary Ann she saw that the young girl was gone.

Dan had been gone for over a month on a job that required his being there. Many years earlier he stopped going on the missions as he started feeling unable to do his job. He was getting older. He left Captain Jim Stae in charge of all missions that God's Angels did.

Terrorism had become a major concern for most larger businesses which gave God's Soldiers a great deal of security work. They were being hired for everything from bodyguard work to running entire security programs for a business. In this job Dan was setting up security for a large oil company and their refineries.

After thirteen years of being on the run from Major Gillis God's Soldiers had built another compound for security reasons and as a base of operation. Because of how far the United States had fallen under the command of a Socialist president many people that had money to do it were fortifying their homes and property.

The God's Soldiers' Compound sat on 127 acres of land far out in the Texas hill country. A small creak ran through the property and into a large lake which banked on the land. Dan and most of those that worked with God's Soldiers enjoyed hunting and this land was full of deer, wild hogs, and squirrels.

Over the next few months Evie and Mary Ann worked with Dan and Sandy to refine some of the abilities that Mary Ann had. She was able to change into a Neanderthal at will and then change back. Anger had nothing to do with it. By just thinking about it she could extend her shield to push things or people away from her. She was also able to cause the ground to crack open a short distance away. The crack would open enough to swallow anything or anyone she wanted. Then she was able to close the crack on whatever or whomever had fallen in.

But for now her personal strength even as a Neanderthal was still that of a nine year old human girl. When her father changed into the beast his strength almost doubled. Maybe this would change in Mary Ann in time.

After loosing all trace of Evie and her daughter a few years earlier Major Gillis had given up on finding them. From time to time he would get a lead only to find out that the story

11

was not true. He also heard stories about the large Neanderthal being seen throughout the United States but he knew these stories were not true either. Nine years earlier he had Michael locked up in their underground holding facility designed for those; special test subjects called Changers.

A Changer was a test subject that had different than human DNA injected into them. This DNA caused them to change into different things depending on the DNA that they were given. None of them excepted the DNA willingly.

Michael and the other Changers were kept sedated to the point that they could not attempt an escape. When Colonel Dillard was taken off of his job at Fort Hood he thought that loosing Michael. In fact he was moved to the underground facility in Northern Oklahoma and put in charge. He got the shock of his life when Lieutenant Pile captured Michael under Major Gillis. So Colonel Dillard still got what he wanted. Each day he walked by the cell that held Michael and smiled. One time he even allowed Michael to come out of the sedation enough to tell him where he was and that he; Colonel Dillard was holding him there. It was just a way to get back at Michael for all of the time spent trying to catch him.

Mary Ann was spending all of her time at home after her actions at the grocery store parking lot. She was not being punished but she had to learn what could happen to her if Major Gillis started looking for them again.

Colonel Briks had made a few changes to the God's Soldiers. He continued the mercenary part of it as he was making a great deal of money from big companies needing security. When he found a person in his group that he could trust he asked them to join his other security force. It involved guarding and watching over Evie and Mary Ann.

Dan believed that God helped him to find Evie and Mary Ann for this reason. He also believed that God helped him to get rich off God's Soldiers so he would have the money to start God's Angels; the security group that took care of Evie and Mary Ann.

As God's Angels guarded the fortress home of Dan and

Sandy Briks they did nothing else. They did no manual labor unless it had to do with improving security around the Compound.

Mary Ann knew that she had to stay on the property but she could walk the back part of the property as long as at least one of God's Angels was with her. All of the neighbors knew that the security on Dan's property carried AR-15s but they were really M-16s. They also carried a pistol of their choice. So with all of the terrorist around Dan's neighbors thought nothing when they saw Mary Ann walking with well armed security close behind her.

Mary Ann loved playing where the creek ran into the lake. That spot was on the back side of the property. Evie also loved fishing there. Like Michael she and Mary Ann loved their fried catfish. But what no one knew was that the back part of the property was being watched.

The neighbor across the fence on the back of the property saw the fuzzy picture of the unknown child that almost looked like a young Neanderthal. He had seen Mary Ann many times playing there and thought that the fuzzy picture looked almost like her. If he could prove that May Ann was a younger Neanderthal that might be the child of the captured Neanderthal then there might be a great deal of money in it for him.

Richard Perkins set up cameras along his fence with the Compound. Only about one third of the Compound's back fence was along the lake leaving Richard plenty of room for cameras. Finally he got enough pictures that he was sure that Mary Ann was or; at least could be, the child of the Neanderthal. God's Angels had no idea what was going on.

God's Angels made regular rounds on the property looking for any trespassers. One day one of them was looking across the fence when she saw a game camera hanging on a tree. That would have been no problem except that this camera was only three feet from the fence and facing the Compound. Who ever owned this camera was not trying to take pictures of deer or wild hogs. There was no doubt that they were watching the

Compound for some reason.

The camera was left alone but the guard took a picture of it with her cell phone and sent it to Colonel Briks. Then she continued her rounds as if she had not seen a thing. Another minute later she found another game camera that was also facing towards the Compound. She took a picture of it and sent it to Briks as well.

Late that evening Dan had a meeting with the members of God's Angels. They decided to go across the fence the next morning and collect all of the cameras that they could find.

Dan wanted to do more but decided that by taking his cameras he might get the hint. He was wanting to confront the land owner across the fence but that could wait. He did not want to cause any attention to be drawn to them at the Compound.

Finding the cameras did not seem to bother Mary Ann but her mother was another story. Evie was almost scared to death that the government had found them but Dan assured her that the government would have been using more sophisticated cameras not game cameras. If they had been discovered then the government would be using satellites or high flying drones to watch the Compound. Evie said that she felt a little better but she still shook from fear for a while. She lost her husband and did not want to loose her daughter as well.

The next morning Dan took a few of his security to the back fence. Once the were at the back of he property they looked around before crossing the fence. Then he kept watch while three others crossed the fence and collected four game cameras; all within five feet of the fence and facing the fence. There was no doubt that the property owner was spying on the Compound. Then they took the camera back to the home where Dan took the chips out and looked at what was on them. As he sat at his computer he saw that the only pictures were of security making their rounds along the fence. Then he did some research and found who owned the land across the fence.

Suddenly there was a loud knock at the door. Because of what was going on Dan had asked Evie and Mary Ann to not answer the door or the phone for a while. The woman that found the cameras answered the door to find a tall man standing there.

"I want to talk to the people that crossed my fence and took my cameras." he insisted.

"That would be me." Dan said as he calmly walked up to the door.

The man pushed his way past the woman who pushed him back outside causing him to fall on the ground. The man started to pull a pistol that was holstered on his side but Dan had his pistol pointed at the man in a split second.

"You had better keep that thing right on your side or I'll kill your ass right now." Dan warned him.

The man slowly moved his hand away from his pistol and the stood. "You missed one camera so I saw your people crossing the fence and taking four of my other cameras."

"Who are you mister?" Dan asked.

"My name is Perkins … Richard Perkins and you stole my cameras."

"Well … Mister Perkins… your cameras … all of them were facing our property." Dan calmly said. "Why was that?"

"I can face my cameras anyplace I want." Richard yelled.

"Listen Mister Perkins." that was all he could say before being interrupted.

"No you listen." this time Richard was cut short as he looked down the barrel of Dan's pistol again.

"Shut up you son of a whore." Dan was tired of Richard's attitude. "You're not getting your cameras back and if we find any more cameras facing our property we will come to your home and visit you." Dan lowered his pistol and added; "And you might not survive the visit. Do you hear me Mister Perkins?"

For the first time since he got there Richard toned his voice down some. "You're not getting away with this … and who are you anyway?"

"My name is none of your business but I am the head of security here." Dan told him. "Now back off or so help me God you will wish you had."

Richard grit his teeth and whipped around without saying another thing. Then he got in his truck and left.

"You should have shot him in the leg or something's warning." Evie said as she walked up behind Dan.

"You can't do that." Dan advised her. "Once you take that first shot you start a feud that can get very nasty and last for years."

Dan and Evie walked back into the kitchen and sat at the table. Dan explained to them how that things had changed. He did not want either of them to go to the back fence anymore; not for a while anyway.

"Mister Perkins is going to be trouble but we can reduce that trouble if nether of you go back to the lake for a while … maybe a long while."

Evie and Mary Ann agreed but Mary Ann already went no place outside without an armed guard anyway.

Mary Ann was smarter than anyone knew. She understood the dangers of the government wanting to find her and this man that was just there could tell them about her. For a while now she had become quiet. This was because of her mind maturing. No one knew it but this maturity was because of the alien DNA that was in her. Although still a child Mary Ann understood everything that was going on.

Richard bought more game cameras and set them up on the same trees that the other ones were on. He wanted Dan to cross the fence again while he sit in hiding with a shotgun. He did not care what this Head of Security wanted. The cameras were on his property and he could do what he wanted; on his property.

Chapter 2

Dangerous Neighbors

Mary Ann's tenth birthday was coming up. She was excited but had no friends to come to any party. Her birthday party would be full of adults. But she also understood that this was her life. It had to be and would be for the rest of her life. With her party still two weeks away Sandy was going crazy with some news of her own.

One morning while Dan, Sandy, and Evie sat around the table drinking their coffee Sandy told her big news. She held Dan's hand and asked if he loved her. She knew he did but just wanted to hear it.

"Of course I do." an told his wife. "You know I do."

With a smile Sandy looked at her husband and then Evie. "I'm gon'a have a baby."

Dan's jaw dropped leaving his mouth open. He was in shock.

"You're gon'a be a Daddy Dan." Evie said. "Hello Daddy."

Sandy reached over and used her hand to close Dan's mouth. Those last words from Evie did not help his being in shock. As hot as it was he raised his cup of coffee and gulped it all down. Then the hot coffee hit him and he snapped back into the real world.

After giving Sandy a kiss he got up and got another cup of coffee. Then without saying a thing he went back to his computer. He wanted to find out as much as he could about Richard. Come to find out Richard had a small but still bad criminal record.

Richard Perkins had been arrested three time for simple assault. His CHL had been revoked but he was still carrying a pistol when he came to the home. This showed Dan that Richard had a violent temper and he needed to be watched. He advised God's Angels that if he ever pointed a firearm at them they were to open fire and kill him.

"Waiting until the man fired first is just plane stupid. This is something a retarded Liberal might do." he told his security. "We already know that this is a violent man so don't take any chances."

Dan had a HAM radio base unit set up in the same room as his computer. The radio was always monitored in case a walking patrol needed help. They used the MUR frequencies which were legal to use without a licenses and his radios had a tone set in them so that anyone else that was listening to that frequency could not hear his security talking.

One day he was working on his computer when one of his security called in on the radio. "Bensy to base." the caller said. "I've been shot."

Sergeant Bensy was the woman that found the first cameras. Bensy went on to say that as she was walking the fence she was shot by someone on the other side of the fence with a shotgun. She was hiding behind an old log but she was seeing no movement.

God's Angels instantly went on alert. All but three of them went to the back of the property where Bensy was. The other three got Evie and Mary Ann in a safe room upstairs. One stayed with them while the other two guarded the front and back door.

When Dan and the others got to Bensy they spread out along the fence. If any shooting started they were to kill who ever it was on the other side of the fence that was doing the shooting.

Dan kneeled beside Bensy and saw that three of the shot from the shotgun blast hit her lower left right leg. The bleeding was bad but the medical team go busy working on her. Dan was mad and stood in defiance of anyone looking across the fence. Then he got on his handheld radio and called the home. The person watching the front door ran into the radio room and answered him.

"Lock the home down." he ordered the person. "We are going to visit our neighbor."

"Yes Sir." the person said. Then he started locking the front

18

and back door.

That was when Dan realized that Sandy had fallowed them to the back fence. He ordered her back to the home where she would be safe.

"I'm part of God's Angels and am well able to do my job." Sandy insisted.

"I know you are but you will fallow orders." Dan said.

"Why are you sending me back and no one else?" she asked him.

"Because they are not carrying my baby." he told her as he gave her a hug. "Now please go back to the house before I have to discipline you."

"Ooooooo!" she said. "Does that mean that you may spank me?"

"Maybe later tonight but please do as I asked you to do."

After kissing her husband on the cheek Sandy turned and walked back to the home. When she got there she manned the radio so that the other guard could go back to watching the front door.

Leaning on the two from the medical team Sergeant Bensy walked back to the home where her wounds were re-cleaned and new bandages were put on her leg. Then she was taken to her room in the barracks that had been built for all of Dan's people.

Dan and the other five with him crossed the fence being careful to watch everything. The shooter could still be out there ready to ambush them. They walked for just about fifty feet when the came to a dirt road through the woods. Dan looked down and saw fresh tire tracks in the dirt and knew that this road would take them back to Richard's home. The problem was; which direction was his home?

Dan asked the other which direction they thought they should go. After a short discussion Dan decided to go to the left. They walked in single file about twenty feet apart from each other. They had only walked about one hundred yards when Dan raised his fist. This was the signal to stop. Someone was driving towards them so he opened his fist with the fingers spread out.

This meant to spread out. Everyone quickly hit the bushes on both sides of he road.

As the truck drove by Dan looked at the driver. It was in fact Richard. He must have been driving back to the fence. Dan figured that he was putting up more cameras but there was no way to know for sure. When they went back they would check fro more cameras and collect them as well. When the truck was out of sight Dan and the others came back out to the road. Then he ordered the others to head back to the fence. There was no reason to confront Richard at his home where he might have friends when they could confront him alone at the fence.

When Dan and the others got back to the fence they saw Richard setting up more cameras. Dan had the others hide in the bushes to watch Richard. Richard set up three cameras this time. He bought all that the feed store had. When Richard finished he went back about forty to fifty feet and sat down against a tree. This time he was carrying a rifle

Richard sat against the tree for a long time. He had no way of knowing when the little girl might comeback but he was now after the Head of Security; Dan. He did not figure that it would be long before seeing that man again and; he was right.

As Richard sat against the large oak tree and watched across the fence he felt cold steal being pushed against the side of his neck.

"Don't move or so help me God I'll pull the trigger." Sergeant Bensy said. "Then I'll cut you up for catfish bate and dry your bones to grind up into bone meal. The okra in the garden will thank you for that."

At that time Dan walked up and took the rifle from Richard. A Ruger 10/22. Nice rifle for a small caliber." Then he tossed the Ruger to one of his security and asked another one to toss him a grenade. "Now Mister Perkins." Dan said. "Why have you set up more cameras and then set out here like you were going to shoot one of us?"

"Because I was going to shoot one of you if you touched my cameras again." Richard said ash looked around. "Just didn't expect you to be sneaking up behind me."

"Mister Perkins." Dan said as he pulled the pin on the grenade. "Surely by now you know that you're outgunned. Just incase you don't know how outgunned you are let me show you something."

Dan asked Sergeant Bensy to fire a few round on full auto. With a big smile on her face she fired about five rounds into the air. Then he tossed the grenade about ten feet away into the lake. Seconds later a flume of water shot into the air with a loud boom.

"Now Mister Perkins ... we will be taking these new cameras and this Ruger 10/22 rifle." Dan calmly advised Richard. If you put up one more camera facing our property then we will becoming back for you. We will burn your home down but leave you alive that it burned down because you're an ass hole. This is your last warning ... Mister Perkins."

Dan and the others crossed back to their side of he fence and took the cameras and rifle with them. Looking back Dan saw Richard getting back into his truck. He watched him long enough to make sure that the man did not come out of the truck with another rifle. When Richard drove off Dan then turned and fallowed his people back to the home.

Dan had one of his security hide the Ruger 10/22 rifle with some of the other illegal weapons like the grenades in case Richard had the police come out to get it. And wouldn't you know it; the next morning the local police was knocking on the front door.

Dan answered the door to find four police officers standing there with Richard behind them.

"He's the one." Richard yelled as he pointed at Dan. "He took my rifle and seven game cameras."

"Mister Perkins." the police sergeant said. "You will be quiet and you will stay outside." Then he looked at Dan and added; "I'm looking for the Head of Security."

"That would be me Sir. I'm Dan Briks." he said as he stepped back and let the police in. "How may I help you?"

"I have a warrant to search this home Sir." the Sergeant

advised.

"You don't need a warrant Sergeant." Dan advised trying to be as polite as possible. "What or who are you looking for?"

Mister Perkins said that you crossed your fence with him and took his rifle from him as he hunted. He also said that you took seven game cameras."

"No Sir. The man is a certifiable nut case." Dan said as he laughed. "My survival group was training yesterday morning when he started yelling at us from across the fence. He was on his side so we ignored him. He did not like that and got louder." Dan took a few steps and then added; "He did mention that someone stole his game cameras but it was probably some kids. I'm sorry Sergeant but we are not going to do anything illegal. We even have permits to carry these M-16s. With these rifles why would I take his little .22 caliber rifle?

"I agree Sir but the judge swore out this warrant so I have to serve it and look around."

"Oh I understand Sir." Dan assured the Sergeant. "I have no problem with you but this guy is a nut case and should not be allowed to own a firearm. I have to admit that I am afraid everything one of my security makes rounds that he might shoot them."

"I'll talk to the judge about that." the Sergeant assured Dan. "But the judge might want to talk with you before he does anything."

"That makes since." Dan replied. "Just let me know."

"I will Sir. The Sergeant said as he shook Dan's hand. "Thank you for your cooperation."

As soon as Dan opened the door Richard was standing in the doorway yelling. "You get my rifle and cameras?"

"We did not find your rifle or your cameras Mister Perkins." the Sergeant said. "Now leave these people alone."

Richard closed his lips so tight they almost started bleeding. Then he yelled out a warning. Looking at Dan he yelled; "This isn't over. You'll be hearing from me again."

"As long as it's done legally Mister Perkins." the Sergeant

advised. But if you keep bothering these people I'll becoming to your home with a warrant."

"Have a nice day Sergeant." Dan said. Then headed; "And you to Mister Perkins."

That just made Richard madder than he already was. He got into his truck and left out the gate behind the police.

"We will be hearing from him again." Dan told everyone there. "This isn't over."

It was quiet for the next two weeks. Mary Ann's birthday party was the next day and everyone was excited; especially Mary Ann. Ten years was a nice rounded number so Mary Ann had been looking forward to this day for almost two full years. It was almost like a right-of-passage for her; a goal that she had set for herself for some reason. But with this goal finally being met what would the next goal be?

On the morning of Mary Ann's birthday she woke up early. Already the birthday gifts covered the dining room table with even few on the kitchen table. As Mary Ann looked at the gifts she saw that all of them were from her mother, Dan, Sandy, and the security there. This only bothered her a little because she had already excepted this as her life. But the one thing that did bother her was that there was nothing from her father.

Mary Ann knew where her father was and why. She did not really expect a gift from him because that would mean that the government knew where she and her mother were. It just hurt her knowing that her father could not be with her on this special day.

Around 10:00 in the morning the party started. Those with God's Angels that were not actually on duty were there. Even a few from God's Soldiers were there. The others were on a mission.

Everyone sang "Happy Birthday" to Mary Ann. Then it was time to open her gifts. Finally she worked her way to a long box wrapped in green paper. Forest green was her favorite color. She tore the paper from the box dropping it on the floor that was already covered with wrapping paper. With the wrapping paper on the floor she read the words on the long box. It was the Ruger 10/22 rifle that she had been wanting ever since she saw the one Dan took from Richard. This was not Richard's rifle as it had been put away. This was a new rifle.

Evie was not all that happy about her little girl having a firearm but ten year old children overseas were killing our soldiers. Therefore; why should she not learn to use a rifle and later, a pistol?

After all of the gifts were open it was time to eat the cake. Evie got the cake which was sitting on the top of the stove and set it on the kitchen table in front of Mary Ann. Instead of having ten tiny candles on top of the cake her mom had placed two candles. One candle was shaped like the number one and the other one was shaped like he number zero. Put side-by-side on the cake they said ten.

Evie had made Mary Ann her favorite cake. It was a three layer chocolate cake with thin layers. Between the layers and on top and around it was a thick coat of rusty red colored Chocolate icing. Evie made it herself. Mary Ann got the first piece but no one ate until after prayer. Once everyone had their piece of cake Evie prayed.

"Thank you Father for bringing us altogether on this day. Thank you for watching over Mary Ann and bring her safely to this day. Please continue to watch over her. You have brought her through a few trials and I know you love her. Evie was quiet for a few seconds and then continued. *Father … please watch over all of us here. Keep us all safe. Thank you Father for everything we have. Amen."*

Mary Ann dug into her piece of cake like she had not eaten for weeks. This cake was her favorite of all cakes. Her favorite dessert was a blueberry cheesecake that her mom also made. But as far as cakes go this chocolate cake her mom made was the best.

Some of the other gifts that Mary Ann got was a doll that she really just had to have, a CD player and a few music CDs, and something that every child loves to get as a gift; clothes. But when the party was over the first thing she wanted to do was shoot her new rifle.

Dan went into the back yard and stapled a target on a large oak stump. Then he stepped off fifty yards and stuck a four foot long piece of PVC pipe in the ground. He took a while explaining everything about the rifle to Mary Ann.

"Remember that this is not a toy. It is a killing tool designed to do one thing ... to kill." Dan explained. "Never point a firearm at anyone even on accident. Always keep in mind where your rifle is pointed."

"Yes Sir." Mary Ann said.

Dan loaded the magazine and showed Mary Ann how to load the magazine into the rifle. Then he chambered a round and handed the rifle to Mary Ann.

As Mary Ann held he rifle Dan said; "Now pay attention. Someday this rifle might save your or your mom's life."

"Yes Sir." Mary Ann acknowledged. "But what makes you think I need a rifle or pistol?"

Dan looked into Mary Ann's eyes and asked; "Is there anything about you that you have not told me?"

"I can do a lot more than you know." she told him. "A lot more."

"Like what?" Dan asked. "Oh I don't know. I'll show you some day."

"You need to show me as soon as you can girl."

"I will." she agreed.

Dan knew that she was not intentionally hiding things from him. Any powers or other abilities that she had that he did not know about was just of no concern to her. It was like drinking a glass of water. No big deal. It was the same as he last glass of water before it. However; this was a big deal to Dan. He needed to keep up on what she was capable of doing.

Mary Ann was right handed so Dan got on his knees on her left side and just behind her some. He helped her to holdup the rifle for a minute and then showed her how to lean her elbow on her stomach to brace the rifle. Then he had her click the safety off and it was time to fire.

Mary Ann took aim at the white target with the black center. Then she fired but missed the black bull's eye by four inches. She fired again and got closer. Then on the third shot she hit the bull's eye. Almost every shot after that hit the black center of he target.

"You're good." Dan encouraged her. "And you'll get better. It just takes time."

"Will I be as good as you?" Mary Ann asked Dan.

"With practice … yes."

As Mary Ann continued to fire her new rifle; what Mary Ann had said earlier bothered him. She admitted that she could do a lot more than he knew she could do. *Was she hiding her abilities for some reason? Not understanding her abilities; could she be dangerous to all of them?* These and other questions went through Dan's mind as he watched this little girl having a blast. She was really getting into shooting this rifle.

Chapter 3

She's Growing Up

When Dan and Mary Ann came back from shooting her new rifle he had one of his security people store the rifle in their rifle vault. As Mary Ann played with her new doll Dan talked with Evie about what Mary Ann had said.

"What else can she do?" Evie asked Dan.

"I don't know but she's very confident with it." Dan explained. "She said that she would tell me about it later."

"No!" Evie said as she stood. "She needs to tell us right now."

Evie went into the den where Mary Ann was playing and asked her to come into the kitchen for a minute. Mary Ann was in her own little world taking care of her baby doll but still answered her mom. She stood but did not forget her doll which she cuddled in one arm pretending to feed it a plastic bottle.

"Yes Mommy?" Mary Ann asked. She was always very respectful.

"Tell me how you did shooting your rifle." Evie broke the ice with that.

"Oh I had fun." Mary Ann said as she lay her doll on the table. Suddenly the rifle was more important. "Uncle Dan said that I shot real good."

With Dan being there all of her life she had been raised calling him Uncle Dan. When he and Sandy got married then she suddenly became Aunt Sandy. She loved them both just as if they were her blood uncle and aunt.

The terrorist and basic criminals were starting to join forces. A few whole cities had been taken over by them. In Texas alone the liberal mayors of Dallas and Fort Worth did nothing about

27

the gangs as they forced their sanctuary city ideas on the good citizens living there. They cared more about the illegals than the citizens there allowing the gangs to take over. One gang ran Dallas while another gang ruled over Fort Worth.

Both gangs answered to a terrorist group. This group called themselves Allah's Right Hand. They supplied weapons and explosives to the gangs and helped them to take over the two cities. But they insisted that the two gangs did not fight each other. The gang leaders agreed. By cooperating with Allah's Right Hand they had become more powerful than they ever expected. Allah's Right Hand also took over Austin and used the gangs in Houston to take over that city.

Larger cities all over the country were being taken over by terrorist from the middle east which used the gangs in those cities as soldiers. The police and city leaders were executed on the spot while police departments were burned to the ground. The gangs had become the police enforcing their own twisted laws on the public.

Fort Hood had also been overrun by Allah's Right Hand using gangs from all around. Almost everyone there that survived the fight was executed anyway. This gave used the Base as a base of operation in the state of Texas.

Washington DC was under siege but holding its ground. Most of the military in that area had moved to the District of Columbia to protect it and the government officials that caused this whole problem. The Socialist President of the United States allowed an open border so terrorist nations in the middle east sent in their soldiers. When there were enough of them they started taking over larger cities.

While the terrorist waited for their numbers to build up they made deals with larger gangs in the cities. The gangs had stopped fighting each other and were organizing themselves. In some cases gangs combined their membership into one gang making them even more powerful. The MS-13 gang in New York City was already out of control because of their being a sanctuary city. Now with the help of the terrorist they ruled with an iron fist killing anyone that got in their way.

This was the result of Socialism and sanctuary cities. Idiots elected Socialist into government offices who allow open borders and sanctuary cities to protect the illegals that crossed the open borders. Their numbers grew while good American citizens were being murdered in record numbers.

Seeing this coming when a socialist was elected as President of the United States two years earlier Dan had started buying and collecting weapons and explosives like never before. He even bought three ATVs and had armor placed on the doors and in front and back. At one point he thought that his two groups were better equipped than the military.

Because things were getting so bad Dan asked Evie and Mary Ann to not go outside but they did not want to stay in the house. He agreed to them going outside as long as they stayed close to the house and had at least one God's Angels with them.

One morning Dan, Sandy, and Evie was sitting on the balcony overlooking the back yard. Quite often they drank their morning coffee there. On this morning a cool breeze blew making it a perfect morning. But just when you start enjoying life someone always comes along to ruin it.

Suddenly there was a pop from the woods and a bullet ricocheted off of the rock side of the house. Instantly Dan grabbed Evie and pulled her down to the floor of the balcony. Sandy returned fire spraying bullets into the trees about one hundred yards away. A second pop was heard and this bullet grazed Sandy's shoulder. Within seconds the rest of God's Angels ran into the woods to find who had fired the shots.

As Dan and Sandy took Evie into her bedroom and into the interior of the home Dan got a call on his hand held radio. No one was found in the woods but they were continuing to the back of the property.

"That bastard." Dan said. "Now he's shooting at us."

Dan walked to the back of the property where he met with the other members of God's Angels. He was mad. He stood there looking around for any hint that Richard had crossed the fence but there was nothing that showed it. He looked into the trees across the fence and again found no one there. Some of the Angels started to cross the fence but he stopped them.

"I'll take care of this." Dan told the Angels. "It's personal now."

When Dan and the Angels got back to the home he found the medic patching up Sandy's shoulder. "She won't be firing a rifle for a week or so but she's okay Sir." Doc told him. Doc was the head of Dan's medical team.

"What are you gon'a do?" Sandy asked Dan.

"I'm not sure yet but I'm not calling the police." he told his wife. "Then again ... I might go talk to the Sergeant but not file any complaints.

Dan cleaned up and put on clean clothes. Then he walked over to the bed where Sandy lay and kissed her good-by. "I'll be right back." he assured her.

"Take someone with you Baby." Sandy begged her man. "I know you can handle anything but you might need someone to calm you down."

Dan went onto the balcony where Sergeant Bensy was trying to dig one of the bullets out from between two rocks that made that side of the house. She pulled it out just as Dan walked up.

"It's a .22 caliber Sir." Bensy told Dan.

"He's got him another .22 caliber rifle." Dan said. "That's why he missed. The distance between the woods and this balcony is to far for accurate shooting with a .22 rifle."

Dan took the bullet and put it in his right pants pocket. If he needed to he might show it to the Sergeant. He went out to his truck which was parked in the back yard and opened the door. Once again he looked into the woods hoping to spot someone but only his security was out there. He had added one more walking patrol that only walked just inside the trees from the back yard. With a heavy sigh he got in his truck and drove out the gate.

When Dan walked into the police department he went straight up to a glass window. On the other side of the window was the police dispatcher.

30

"May I help you Sir?" the dispatcher asked.

"I need to talk to one of your sergeants but I don't know his name." Dan was embarrassed that he drove all the way down there and did not even know the Sergeant's name.

"Maybe Sergeant O'Neil can help you." the dispatcher advised. "Please sit over on the bench and he will be right out."

Dan sat there for about ten minutes before he heard a familiar voice. "Good morning Mister Briks."

Dan stood and shook the Sergeant's hand. Then he fallowed Sergeant O'Neil to his office. As both men sat down O'Neil asked Dan what he needed.

"I'm not filing a complaint because there is no evidence but I did want to talk with you about this." Dan said. "You see Sergeant … I'm responsible for the lives of a woman and her ten year old daughter out there. This morning someone in the trees about one hundred yards from the back of the home fired two shots … one of which grazed my wife's shoulder. She's pregnant right now too."

"And you don't want to file a report?" O'Neil asked. "Why not?"

Dan reached into his pocket and pulled out the bullet from the home and tossed it on O'Neil's desk. "That's one of the bullets. I'm taking care of this himself."

"Don't take the law into your own hands Dan." O'Neil urged him.

"Oh I'm not." Dan assured him. "I added a 24/7 walking patrol in the woods there."

"So if you're not filing a formal complaint then why are you here?" O'Neil asked.

"I think Mister Perkins fired those two shots." he said. "That's a .22 caliber bullet not the bullet from a sniper's rifle."

O'Neil looked at the bullet. "It's a .22 bullet alright but Mister Perkins could not have fired it."

"Why not?"

He was arrested two nights ago for a traffic fine he didn't pay. It went to a warrant and we went and picked him up two nights ago."

"Then who would shoot at us from back there and with a .22 rifle?"

"I don't know Dan but I still urge you to file that complaint."

"Why?" Dan asked. "Nothing personal but ... what can you do?"

O'Neil sat there with no answers to give Dan. Dan got up and shook O'Neil's hand and then grabbed the bullet. Placing the bullet in his pants pocket he wished O'Neil a good day and left.

Just as Dan started to walk out of the building O'Neil yelled and stopped him. "I need to let you know something that might be of some interest." the two sat on the bench as O'Neil continued. "The gangs and terrorist that took over Dallas and Forth Worth know that there is not enough of them to spread out and take over smaller surrounding towns. So the gangs are going out and causing as much destruction and problems that they can in order to keep us all off balance. Maybe one of them fired those two shots.

"Then I'm telling my security to kill anyone on the property that is not one of us and carrying a firearm." Dan insisted.

O'Neil let out a heavy sigh and said; "Well ... lets just say that I didn't hear that. Times are getting really bad in this country. Thanks to that son of a whore socialist president we have we almost don't even have country anymore. Those liberal bastards have destroyed this country. That's been their goal for many years. I used to say that they were going to destroy this country. Now they're almost finished doing just that."

"I know." Dan agreed. "I've seen it coming for a long time."

"Dan ..." O'Neil said. "You do what ever you feel you have to do out there. Just try to keep it legal."

"I'll do that." Dan promised. Then he stood and shook O'Neil's hand again and left. As he walked out to his truck he thought about what all he was going to do. He knew that he had to make some changes and some of those living at his home may not like those changes. But if they were to survive the changes going on around them then they would have to do as he wished.

He was the boss and if anything else it was his home with Evie paying for a few things. Then he rethought what he wanted. The home was his but Evie and little Mary Ann owned part of it too. It was their home too.

As Dan drove home he was in his own little world. He stopped for stop signs and red lights and slowed through the school zone. He was alert enough to do all of those things but if someone was to slap him he might not even know it. He worried for Evie and little Mary Ann and for his wife and unborn baby. And now with the country going to hell he was getting older. What was he doing having a baby at his age anyway?

Dan finally woke up from his daydream when he realized that he was sitting in his truck with the transmission in park. He looked to his left and saw Mary Ann coming out of the home to him. She smiled and then suddenly there was a loud pop to his right.

Dan looked out of the right side door window just in time to get a face full of shattered glass. Who ever shot at them earlier was back out there. He jumped out of the truck and tackled Mary Ann. There was another pop and he felt the bullet hit him in the butt but Mary Ann was safe and that was all he cared about at that time. The person doing the shooting had to have shot him under the truck. Two more pops were heard and Dan could hear the bullets ripping through the truck door.

Then Mary Ann stood and when Dan looked in her face it was clear that she was not Mary Ann anymore. She had changed into an almost five foot tall Neanderthal child; mean as a wounded wolf. She walked around the truck and let our a roar that would have scared her father. Dan could even feel the truck shaking. Then she let out another roar and thrust her hands out in front of her. The grass in front of her lay down as if it was being pushed over. Suddenly the trees many yards away began to explode as if tons of explosives had been set on them all and blown up.

"Mary Ann." Evie yelled at her daughter.

That was enough to get the young Neanderthal to calm down.

In seconds Mary Ann was back to being Mary Ann. She calmly walked back to Dan and asked if he was okay.

"I am now … thanks to you." he said as tears flowed down his cheek. He was so proud of her.

The medical team carried Dan into the home where they lay him on the table. Doc saw that the wound was more than he wanted to attempt so he called an ambulance. God's Angels searched the trees that had been destroyed and found a young man of about seventeen years of age. He was dead from the blast of the exploding trees. Shards of wood from the trees covered his body. They also found the security person that was on foot patrol in the woods. Someone had come up behind him and slit his throat. A bloody knife was fond sheathed and on the young man's side.

The police were called and Sergeant O'Neil came out there as well. He looked around and then walked into the house. Dan was on the gurney being strapped down for his trip to the hospital.

"Ha O'Neil." Dan said with his hand stretch out.

O'Neil shook his hand and then said that it looked like self defense to him. "But what caused those treed to blow up out there." he asked Dan. "You don't have explosives out here do you?"

"Of course not Sergeant." he said with a smile. "I wouldn't do that. It's against the law to have explosives."

"I still have to explain finding the young man in those … blown up trees."

"I guess that boy brought more than just a rifle." Dan explained. "To bad he's dead. Now you can't ask him.

O'Neil's mouth hung open for a few seconds. "I guess that boy must have been carrying a lot of explosives."

"He must have wanted to blow this place up too." Dan explained.

O'Neil thought for a moment and then added; "That's what my report's going to say."

"We need to go Sir." the EMT told O'Neil.

"Of course." O'Neil acknowledged. "He's all yours."

As the ambulance drove away O'Neil walked into the kitchen where Evie was talking to Mary Ann. "Just make sure you don't change …" she stopped as O'Neil walked in.

"What do you mean; "she can't change"?

"Oh …" Evie was not sure what to say. "She shouldn't change clothes and just get something else dirty."

"Oh!" He replied. "I need to go but if you all need anything just call me."

Evie got up and walked O'Neil to the front door. "Who was that boy anyway?" she asked.

"I don't know but we'll find out." he assured her.

"Let us know will you?"

"I will."

Evie stood outside as she watched O'Neil drive away. She worried about the boy being killed but more about Mary Ann. This was her first time to kill anyone and she knew that this boy would not be the last. She was so much like her father and that worried Evie.

Mary Ann understood the significance of her changing but she felt that she had to do it. And then when Dan got shot as he protected her it was time to act. It was time to show him and the others what she already knew about herself.

Evie walked back into the home and into the kitchen where Mary Ann was waiting for her. After sitting down she began to question her daughter.

"Am I in trouble Mommy?" Mary Ann asked with an ever so sad look on her face.

"No Baby." she assured the scared little girl. "This is a part of you. In fact you actually did pretty well."

"But … I killed that boy didn't I?"

"He was trying to kill us Baby. The only thing you need to remember is that sometimes you cannot just change to help someone."

"What do you mean?" Mary Ann asked.

"Remember when you changed at the store and opened the

ground to swallow that man's car?"

"Yes Ma'am."

"Well … you should not have done that." Evie tried to explain. "No one's life was in danger and a woman took your picture. Luckily the picture was fuzzy."

"So if someone is about to die then I can … I should help?"

"Let me put it this way. At your age try not to change at all. Now if this happens again then that is okay. Everyone here knows about you. The public must never see you as … me and your father used to call it the beast."

"I think I understand now Mommy." Mary Ann said. "Until I get older I must not change into … the beast … unless I am here."

"And even then not unless you are sure that you can help."

"Okay Mommy."

"By the way." Evie said. "How did you make those trees explode?"

"I saw the man … the boy out there and he was aiming his rifle at us. I just thought about my shield and pushed it to the trees. Then I let loose with some … I think energy from me … and the trees exploded. I was not afraid until then but it scared me."

"Okay Baby. That's all but tell me anytime you discover any new abilities okay?"

"Yes Ma'am."

Chapter 4

A New Friend

Dan was taken to the local hospital. By time he arrived in the ambulance Sandy was already there. She left the home before the ambulance did. He was patched and thn taken to a small recovery room. Sandy was right behind him.

The one bullet that hit Dan in the butt went deep and lay against his tailbone. As he lay on the gurney still knocked out Sandy held his hand. This was her man; the father of her unborn baby.

Suddenly Sandy wished that he did not have a mercenary group. But with so many terrorist in the country, leading a security group was almost as dangerous. If this bullet had hit him just six inches higher then it would have hit his spinal column and he could have been paralyzed for life.

That was when Sandy realized that she had worn her pistol into the hospital. It was covered and hard to see but she was not sure if it was legal to carry in a hospital. She stood to take the pistol out to their truck when O'Neil walked into the room.

"How's he doing?" O'Neil asked.

"The doctor said that he would be going home soon after waking up." Sandy said. "That's all I know."

With O'Neil being a cop he was always investigating things. "When I was at the house Evie told Mary Ann to … I think she asked the girl to be careful when she changed." He told Sandy. "What do you think she meant?"

"I haven idea Sir."

"So it's Sir now." O'Neil mentioned. "Before leaving I could tell that the girl did not like me asking her mother questions. Then I noticed that her left arm had long dark black hair on it."

"You've been drinking on duty." Sandy said as she laughed.

"Yeah well … the other arm looked normal for a young girl."

"You must have seen a shadow over her arm."

"I know what I saw Sandy."

"Sergeant O'Neil …" Sandy said and then swallowed the lump in her throat. "You really need to talk to no one about that until you talk to Dan."

"Talk to me about what?" Dan was barely able to say. He was still under the effects of being knocked out for his surgery.

"We can talk tomorrow Dan." O'Neil advised Dan. "I'll come by the house in the morning. I don't think you're going to feel like coming to see me."

Dan only caught part of what O'Neil said before passing out again. "I'll tell him." Sandy said.

"Good enough." O'Neil said as he turned to leave. Then he looked back at Sandy. "No one is in any trouble. It's just that I am a cop with questions. I like to think that we are all friends but I am a cop first." With a big smile headed; "See you two … and Evie … in the morning."

"I'll have some coffee waiting for you."

"Sounds great. You make great coffee." O'Neil said as he turned and left the recovery room.

Dan woke up again a few minutes later but hospitals like to keep you as long as they can. If they keep you past noon then you have to pay for another day. With that in mind Dan was released just after three in the evening. It is customary to be wheeled out to your vehicle in a wheelchair but Dan could not sit in one. Two male interns had to help him slowly walk to the truck waiting for him.

All of the way home Dan could feel every crack in the road and the potholes were agonizing. If Sandy drove over a feather he knew it. When she pulled the truck in the driveway Dan was reminded with every shake and shimmer of the truck that he needed to get someone working on leveling the driveway. Finally they reached the back of the home and the truck stopped.

"Thank God that's over." Dan said as he looked at Sandy. She was smiling but he knew that she was laughing inside.

Dan had no shortage of people helping him into the home where he went straight to the bedroom and lay down. He could not sit in a chair yet; especially not after that drive home. Sandy gave him a few pain pills and then left for the pharmacy. Dan just wanted to get home and into bed so they came straight home. As soon as Dan fell asleep again Sandy left for the pharmacy to have his pain reliever prescription filled.

After Sandy left it was all quiet in the home; especially upstairs where Dan was. Mary Ann was playing with her new doll in the den when she started thinking about her Uncle Dan. She looked up the staircase knowing that Dan was asleep but that he was all alone. After picking up her doll she went upstairs and into Dan and Sandy's bedroom. Then she pulled a chair beside the bed where Dan was asleep and sat down.

After a while Mary Ann got up and walked out on the balcony. Dan and Sandy's bedroom and Evie's bedroom shared the balcony. She looked out over the large back yard. The lawn care company was there that day taking care of the lawn and flower beds. Two riding lawnmowers were busy with the back yard. Below the balcony a woman worked on the flower bed. Evie had asked her to remove the old flowers so she could plant a few heads of cabbage and some onions. Dan liked his jalapeno peppers so she was going to grow one or two of those plants as well.

Mary Ann looked at the trees that she had destroyed. A tree trimming company was out there cutting the oaks up into firewood for the winter. They had two splitters going splitting the larger pieces into manageable firewood. One thing was for sure. They would have plenty of firewood that winter and maybe for the fallowing two or three years.

Mary Ann heard the TV in Dan's bedroom come on so she went back into the room.

"Well howdy Beautiful." Dan said to Mary Ann.

"Hi Uncle Dan." she said as she ran back to her chair. Pulling the chair against the bed she asked; "You feeling any better?"

"Not really but I'll be okay." he told her." It takes time for the body to heal and the worse you're hurt the longer it takes to completely heal."

"Well no one is going to hurt you while I'm here." Mary Ann said with all of the confidence in the world.

Dan smiled and said; "I believe that."

"I love you Uncle Dan." Mary Ann said.

"I love you too baby girl."

"You're gon'a have to stop calling me that someday." she reminded Dan. "I'm not a baby anymore."

"No you're not." he said as he yawned. "No you're not."

Dan fell asleep again holding Mary Ann's hand. For a long time she stayed right there with her hand in his. Then she heard her mom calling her. She slowly slid her hand out of Dan's hand and stood beside the bed looking at her uncle. With a smile she slid her doll under the sheet beside Dan. Then she went downstairs to her mom.

"Yes Mommy." Mary Ann said as she walked down the stairs.

"Be quiet Baby." Evie told her." Don't wake up your Uncle Dan."

"Oh we talked for a while but he's asleep again."

Evie asked Mary Ann to fallow her into the kitchen. Sandy had already come back and had to quickly talk to Evie and Mary Ann. After they sat down at the table Evie told her daughter that the Sergeant was coming to talk to Dan the next day.

"I like him." Mary Ann said.

Evie and Sandy looked at each other and then back at Mary Ann.

"But he talked with Dan and me at the hospital and said that he got the feeling this morning that you did not like him." Sandy said. "He also saw that one of your arms had long black hair on it but the other one looked normal."

"I was trying to see if I could do it."

"That's what I was talking about earlier Baby." Evie reminded her. "You can't keep doing things like that in front of people. If the government finds us we will be locked up and we will never see each other again."

Mary Ann looked at her mom with tears flowing down her cheek. "I'm sorry Mommy."

"You have got to keep remembering that ... at all times." Evie told her. When O'Neil gets here tomorrow you need to do nothing. You cannot even change your arm ... not even a finger."

"Okay Mommy."

The rest of the day was uneventful. The lawn company finished just before dinner and the tree trimming company stopped working just before dark. There was enough trees to clear and cut into firewood to keep them busy for over a week.

That night Evie and Mary Ann sat on the couch in the den watching the TV. As they watched the local news they learned that the young boy that was killed out in the trees was the nephew of Richard Perkins who was serving one week in jail for a traffic fine that he did not pay. He was being released in two days.

"Is that the man that had all of those cameras back there?" Mary Ann asked her mom.

"That's him."

"Uncle Dan wants to hurt him." Mary Ann replied.

"Now what makes you say that?" Evie wondered.

"I can feel it when I'm around him."

"Is this another ability of yours?"

"I don't know. Sometimes I can tell what someone is thinking but not all the time."

"What am I thinking?" Evie asked.

"Oh I can't just do it Mommy." Mary Ann said. "It just happens sometimes when I'm around someone."

"I think that's another ability of your's ... probably from the alien DNA your father got."

Mary Ann was fully aware of what the government did to her father and then they locked him up because he scared them. She knew that she had alien and Neanderthal DNA in her blood and that she was discovering abilities that her father never had or just

41

did not know he had. She knew all about her father but she never met him. At just ten years old she wanted nothing more than to find her father and break him out of the prison the government had him in. *Maybe when I'm older.* she thought to herself many times. *I'll get my dad when I'm older.*

Everyone in the home slept soundly that night as security made their rounds. At one time around midnight security had an alert to movement in the woods but come to find out it was just a few deer. The large back yard had been planted with grass that, thanks to the lawn company stayed green. Almost every night deer could be seen out there eating the grass. The work being done with the trees was changing the routine of the deer for a while.

The next morning Mary Ann played with her doll in the back yard with two members of God's Angels watching over her. The Angels carried their usual M-16 rifles and pistols of their choice. Another foot patrol was just inside the tree line making their rounds there. When the tree trimmers showed up another foot patrol was added just to make sure that none of them tried hurting anyone. In this day and time no one outside the Compound was trusted.

Around ten in the morning O'Neil drove up and got out of his car. He knocked on the door but no one answered. Thinking that something could be wrong he pulled his pistol. Suddenly the front door opened and he found an M-16 staring him down.

As he looked down the barrel of the rifle he said; "I'm Sergeant O'Neil." He raised his hands.

Sergeant Bensy lowered her rifle and said; "Yes Sir. I recognize you now."

"I thought that I was a goner." O'Neil told Bensy.

"I'm sorry Sir." Bensy said. "I just saw a man with a pulled pistol and it took me a second to recognize you."

"No problems here." O'Neil added. "Of course I'll need to change my pants when I get back but …"

"The others are in the back Sir." Bensy said as she smiled at his comment.

O'Neil walked through the house looking around and then into the kitchen.   "There you all are." he said. "Is Dan still in bed?"

"Yes Sir but he wanted me to wake him up if he was asleep when you got here." Sandy advised.

Sandy and Evie took O'Neil up to the bedroom but Dan was awake and watching the TV. When they walked into the bedroom he turned the TV off.

"Well hello Sergeant." Dan said. "I hear you have a few questions."

"First of all ... how are you doing?" O'Neil asked as he stepped towards Dan and shook his hand.

"I could probably get up but why should I when I have so many people waiting on me hand and foot?"

"Okay then ..." Sandy said. "That's the last glass of water I bring you."

"Oh Babe."

"Your wife and I talked a little at the hospital yesterday and I asked her about something I saw here when I was wrapping up my investigation."

"Yes Sir. She told me."

"So can you explain what I saw?"

"Like she said." Dan was not convincing. "It had to have been shadows."

"There were no shadows Mister Briks. I know what I saw."

"It has nothing to do with what happened yesterday." Dan advised. "You're asking to many questions."

Dan thought for a moment and then asked Evie to go get Mary Ann. When she was gone Dan started explaining a few things. He told O'Neil what really happened but the sergeant was not sure if he should believe the story. When Evie and Mary Ann got up to the room Dan asked Mary Ann to come to him.

With him holding Mary Ann's hand he said; "The Sergeant here is our friend. We told you to never change even a little in font of anyone not living here ... remember?"

"I remember Uncle Dan." Mary Ann did not know what was

going on and was scared.

"I told Sergeant O'Neil here what really happened. It is time that we need to let him know about you so he can help protect us. Do you understand?"

"Yes Sir." she agreed. "What do you want me for?"

"I need you to trust me and show him what you can change into."

Mary Ann looked at her mom.

"Go ahead Baby. This is very important."

Mary Ann nodded her head in agreement and then stepped back a few steps. Then she began to slowly change. Within seconds she was the young Neanderthal child that everyone there loved. Her eyebrows were long and thick and the muscle under them puffed outward. Hair grew on her arms, hands, and legs. Her jaw grew outward slightly.

"My God." O'Neil said.

"You remember about ten years ago the tales about a large Neanderthal?"

"Yes ... I remember but ... I thought that some of the stories were fake." O'Neil was in shock at what he was looking at.

"That Neanderthal is real and this child is his child."

"Change back now Baby." her mom advised her.

Dan told the whole story about where Michael was being held and how they all got there in that home. "Now do you understand why we are so secretive around here?" he asked O'Neil.

"I do now."

"And of course you cannot tell anyone what you saw today." Evie said.

"Of course not." he agreed. If the word got out then my little town would be a mess." He thought for a moment and added. "The terrorist and gangs in Dallas and Fort Worth would love to get their hands on her. Oh my God that would be a headache."

If you want to start a war in your ... little town ... then just let anyone at all know what you saw here."

"No ... no ... no." O'Neil said. "We can't have that."

O'Neil swore to keep this news a secret. He knew that if

anyone on the outside found out about little Mary Ann the consequences would be disastrous in so many ways.

O'Neil walked over to Mary Ann. Kneeling beside her he said; "Now your secret … is my secret too."

Mary Ann smiled and gave O'Neil a big hug and told him that he was now her buddy.

O'Neil stood and stepped back over to Dan. After shaking Dan's hand he then told them all that he had to go. Then he left the room and walked down to his car. Before getting in his car he looked back at the home. A few minutes earlier he thought that he knew all that was going on in his community but now he knew so much more.

As O'Neil drove out the driveway he remembered how he was glued to the TV every time news came on about the Neanderthal. That was ten years earlier. He had always wondered if the Neanderthal was good or bad but he always believed that the creature was real. Now he had met the Neanderthal's daughter. The experience was much more than just pleasurable. Meeting Mary Ann was an honor.

"Are you sure we can trust him to keep this secret?" Evie asked Dan.

Dan thought for a moment and then said; "I do. I really do."

O'Neil drove back to his office at the police department. As he walked into his office he tossed his ball cap at the bent nail on the wall like he had done hundreds of times before. The back of the cap hooked the nail perfectly and hung there on the wall. He was starting to get pretty good at this.

O'Neil sat in his chair behind his desk and looked at his right hand. The Neanderthal had become a kind of hero for millions of people ten years earlier. O'Neil was just one of them. Back then hundreds of Neanderthal clubs formed all over the country. Those were his college years and he was in one such club on campus. He might never have met the Neanderthal but he had met the Neanderthal's daughter and he could tell no one about it. His silence was a small price to pay for the pleasure of knowing; Mary Ann.

Chapter 5

Kidnaped

Richard Perkins was released from jail after serving his time. He was mad over his nephew being killed on Dan's property. It did not matter that his nephew was shooting a rifle at Dan's home he did not believe that his nephew was trying to kill anyone. In his demented mind he saw that his nephew did nothing wrong.

His nephew's mother, his sister, died a few years earlier but his father was still alive. The father and brother came down to get the boy's body to bury him. After the funeral they talked with Richard about what happened. Of course they only got Richard's side of the story. Richard's brother-in-law was mad. His name was Frank and Jessie was now his only son still alive.

"I tried attacking them myself and almost got killed for my troubles." Richard advised. "They have security out there that carries M-16s."

"I want to avenge my son's death." Frank said. "They killed my son and …"

"I know Frank." Richard interrupted him. "But we cannot go in there like I did. They'll kill all of us."

"You have an idea don't you." Jessie asked.

"Yes I do." Richard advised. "We're going to let someone else wipe them all out for us."

"How?" Frank asked.

"I think that little girl could be the daughter of the Neanderthal we knew about ten years ago."

"I remember him." Jessie said. "I was just a kid but I remember listening to stories about him. This girl is his daughter?"

"I think she is." Richard said with smile. "It's a fuzzy picture but a woman took the girl's picture when she turned into a small … Neanderthal."

"If it's a fuzzy picture then how can you be sure it is a Neanderthal child?"

I just believe." Richard admitted.

Richard showed Frank and Jessie the picture. It was the same picture that the woman had taken of Mary Ann at the grocery store. Richard got it online from a local TV station's web site. He made the picture smaller making it clearer to see. By using magnifying glass he was able to see a clearer picture of a young Neanderthal child.

"So how is this going to help us get even?" Frank asked.

"We give this information to a gang in Dallas or Fort Worth and let them go after Dan and his group."

Frank and Jessie were quiet for a few moments as they thought about Richard's plan. "How much would we charge them for this?" Jessie asked.

"Nothing." Richard said. "We give it to them. If we try to make money off of this we might be killed after they get the information. Do you really think gangs have much money? When they wipe out Dan and his group and take that girl away … that will be our payment."

The three men agreed to leave for Dallas the next morning and try to find one of the gangs. The problem was getting past the police blockades. Even if they made it past the police would the gang try to fight their way past the police? Would capturing the child of the Neanderthal be worth it? There was no way to know for sure but they had to try.

The next day the three men drove up Interstate 35 towards Fort Worth. A couple of miles before reaching the loop around Dallas and Forth Worth they came to a roadblock. The public was able to drive on the loop but all exits into the two cities were blocked off by the military. You could exit the loop but turning into the city was impossible. You could only turn away from the two cities. Not being able to reach their goal the men headed back south and talked about what they could do. They finally agreed to drive to Austin.

After reaching Austin the three men found themselves at another roadblock. They turned west off of the interstate and drove a few miles where they found a way to cross into the city of Austin unnoticed. It did not take long to be forced to the side of the road by gang members in a bigger pick-up truck.

Two gang members jumped out of their truck with pistols. A third one carried an AK-47. They ordered Richard, Frank, and Jessie out of the truck. As they got out Richard yelled asking if they were with the Texas Syndicate. The gang members stopped and looked at each other.

"Yes." the leader of the three yelled. "What's it to you?"

"We are here to give your leader some information." Richard said. "The information would mean a great deal to him and … it won't cost him a thing."

"What is this information?" the gang leader asked.

"Naaaaaa! I'm not telling you." Richard said. "I tell you and you kill us and you get the credit for the information. We want to go home."

The leader of the group smiled. "You're smart. I like you." He said with a smile. "Let's go see Bacho. He's our leader. Get in your truck and fallow us but … if you leave from behind us we will find and kill all of you."

"I agree to fallow you." Richard agreed.

Richard fallowed the gang member's truck until they came to a large home. As Richard and the other two got out of the truck they were ordered to stay at the truck. The leader ran into the home while the other two gang members stood by to make sure that they did not leave. A few minutes later the leader of the three that brought them in yelled. Bacho would see them.

The two gang members that were watching over them lead the three up to the house. When they got to the top of the steps the leader of the three gang members opened the front door and let them in.

"Fallow me and remember to never look straight into his eyes." the leader said. "Bacho doesn't like that." Then he added;

"And it is always *Yes Sir* and *No Sir*. Understand?"

"Yes." Richard agreed.

A minutes later Richard, Frank, and Jessie were standing in front of Bacho. Bacho sat behind a large oak desk.

"I was told that you have some information for me. If this information is good then you will leave on your own. If it is not good then you will be carried out of here … dead."

"The information is very good for you Mister Bacho." Richard said.

"Okay then. Tell me this information."

Mister Bacho … do you remember hearing about the Neanderthal about ten years ago?"

Yes but I did not believe the stories." Bacho said with a smile. "They said that it was a promotion for a movie."

"Did you ever see or even hear of the movie showing?"

"No!" Bacho was suddenly interested now. "Go ahead."

"I know that this Neanderthal is real because I have seen him." Richard lied through his teeth. "And here is the picture of what I think is his daughter." Richard handed the picture and magnifying glass to Bacho.

Bacho's eyes got big as he looked at the picture. "I see what you mean but how can this help me?"

"Maybe you could kidnap her and convince her that you're helping her. What would she do to help if she thought that you were helping her mother?

Bacho thought for a minute. "How many men would I need to do this?"

"I don't know." Richard said. "He has about fifteen to twenty security there and they all carry M-16s."

"We would have to separate the girl from her mother before she used her powers to harm us. I take it that she has the same powers her father had?"

"Even more." Richard assured him.

"This is good information." Bacho said. "What do I own you."

"Nothing Sir. Getting rid of them is all the payment I want."

49

Richard said. "I do need to get you there to show you their land and maybe more pictures of the girl."

Bacho decided to take a city buss that they had stolen a few days earlier. In it he would have thirty of his best members. This still left a good thirty to maintain control over the city of Austin. He had hoped to return with the girl before the Texas Mexican Mafia gang attacked them again. The two gangs had been fighting for many years. Allah's Right Hand terrorist group wanted them to stop fighting each other but The Mexican Mafia would not stop. Therefore the terrorist group stopped helping the Mexican Mafia and helped the Texas Syndicate only. This helped the Texas Syndicate to send the Mexican Mafia on the run.

Later that evening Richard, Frank, and Jessie got into their truck to lead Bacho and his Texas Syndicate out of the city using the same rout they used coming in. When it got dark they left out. Within thirty minutes they were all heading north on Interstate 35 away from Austin. Before midnight Richard and the bus drove into his driveway. He set up Bacho and his men for the night and fed them all bar-b-q which Some friends of Richard's had prepared just for them. They would then rest until daybreak when Richard would walk Bacho and his men to his back fence which was also Dan's back fence.

The thirty gang members slept where ever they could find a place to lay down. Bacho slept in one of the two other bedrooms in Richard's home. Around five in the morning Richard got up and made coffee. He had to make four pots of coffee for all that also got up early. Bacho got up just before five in the morning and quickly got himself a cup of the coffee. Then he sat down at the kitchen table with Richard and Frank.

"Thanks for the bed last night." Bacho told Richard. "I can't remember sleeping so good all night. At the home in Austin I wake up every time I hear a gun shot. I never know when the Mexican Mafia is attacking us."

"So they give you a lot of trouble?"

"Not so much anymore." Bacho commented. "Now tell me what we are doing today."

"I'm going to take you through the woods to the fence between me and Dan." Richard said. "The land is his and he is also the Head of Security there."

"And all of his security carry M-16s?"

"Yes Sir."

"And there's about twenty of them?" Bacho asked.

"Fifteen to twenty of them."

"No problem." Bacho said calmly. "We were outnumbered at least two to one when we chased the Texas Mexican Mafia out of Austin."

When it was daylight enough to be able to see Richard lead Bacho and a couple of his men to the back fence. Richard had suggested that he did not take all of his men this time. Just over thirty minutes later they came to the back fence.

"Get down." Richard quietly told Bacho.

Richard pointed at one of Dan's security making his rounds along the back fence. Bacho watched the man slowly walking along the fence looking at everything. Every now and then he would look over the fence and into the trees on Richard's property.

"I wish I had a few of him in my gang." Bacho commented about the security walking in front of them. "He's very watchful and observant."

"I think the woods between this fence and the home is full of security." Richard advised.

"Then maybe we should come in through the front door." Bacho said with a smile.

Richard, Bacho, and the others went back to Richard's home to plan the attack. Richard took Bacho around to the front of Dan's home so he could see what it looked like.

"Big home." Bacho said. "He must also have money around the home."

"Probably but … I don't know."

When Richard and Bacho got back to Richard's home Richard left Bacho and his men in the kitchen to plan their attack. Richard, Frank, and Jessie went into the den and watched

51

the TV.

Bacho and his top soldiers planned their attack for almost three hours. When the planning was over Bacho told Richard that they would go that evening. With only a few hours before mounting the attack on the Compound Bacho's men got the bus ready. They would go in as a lost tourist group. Bacho would need to barrow some nice clothes from Frank though. He and Frank were about the same size.

Later that evening Bacho and his men got on the bus. Bacho drove around to the driveway of Dan's home. That was when he realized that the driveway was to small for turning the bus into. He continued down the road and modified his plans to come back after dark. That way they could park the bus on the road. Then the men could unload and run up to the home in the dark.

When it was finally got dark Bacho drove the bus to within a few yards of the driveway. Trees along the road hid the buss from any eyes at the home. Bacho got off of the bus and looked around. He had already turned the lights off on the bus to keep from drawing attention. When he was sure that it was clear he waved and the others got off of the bus and lined up beside the it. With another wave of Bacho's hand his men ran towards the home.

With his men lined up in front of Dan's home Bacho knocked on the front door. One of the security opened the door and Bacho rushed inside with most of his men behind him. As the others ran around the sides of the home to the back yard security started firing at them. The element of surprise was gone.

An alarm went off waking up everyone in God's Soldiers and God's Angels not to mention any close neighbors. The gun battle raged outside. Some of the gang members rushed into the barracks opening fire on all of the men and women jumping out of bed.

Inside the home Bacho and his men ran upstairs and into the bedroom where Evie and Mary Ann were. Before Mary Ann could do anything Bacho injected her with something that knocked her out. A rifle butt to the side of Evie's face knocked her out.

"Don't hurt her." Bacho insisted slapping the man that hit her. "We need her for that film."

Both Evie and Mary Ann were placed on the buss. Then Bacho and his men left and headed back to Austin. Bacho injected Evie with the same sedation that he gave Mary Ann. A few hours later the bus drove into Austin using the same back roads they left on. None of them were being watched by the police or military.

Mary Ann was taken to the main home of Bacho while Evie was taken to the home next door. Mary Ann was taken to a bedroom where she was chained to the bed. Handcuffs were put around one of her ankles with a three foot long small chain attached to it. The other end of the chain was wrapped around the bedpost and padlocked there. Evie was taken to a bedroom in the home next door and chained to the bed in the same manner.

Back at the Compound the police had been called by neighbors hearing all of the gunfire. O'Neil walked up to Dan who had two bullet holes in his abdomen.

"They said that you'll be okay." he told Dan.

"What about Evie and littler Mary Ann?" he asked O'Neil.

"They seem to be missing." O'Neil advised him as Sandy held her husband's hand.

Sandy had only been shot on the foot one time so she was able to hold Dan who was shot in bed. With her foot hanging off of the bed blood dripped onto the floor from her foot. She loved him very much.

Dan passed out and was loaded on a gurney and strapped down. Then he and Sandy were taken outside and put in the ambulance and were taken to the hospital.

Seventeen of God's Angels were killed and twenty four of God's Soldiers were dead. Those in God's Soldiers that were able to work joined with God's Angels to keep the home secure. Four people of the two groups were also sent to the hospital with bad wounds. From the time that Bacho knocked on the front door until the bus drove away was only seventeen minutes. The Texas Syndicate was more organized than anyone thought.

"God ... help me. I've failed everyone. Please watch over Mary Ann and Evie." Dan whispered with his eyes closed. *"Thank you for watching over me and Sandy."*

Sandy looked down at her husband and heard his prayer. She started to cry and held his hand all the way to the hospital.

When the ambulance got to the hospital Dan and Sandy were taken inside but Dan was rushed straight into the operating room. Sandy was taken to an examination room. She was given a local shot to deaden her foot. As her foot got numb a nurse cleaned her wound. It was not bad as it just barely grazed the bone on the inside of her arch. A doctor came in and stitched up her foot using six stitches. Because the bone had been hit he put a brace on her foot. The padded brace covered the bottom of her foot and came up on the sides. It was wrapped with an ace bandage to hold it tight.

Dan was in surgery for one and a half hours. The damage to his abdomen was not real bad but there was a mess inside to clean up. When the operation was over he was taken to a recovery room. Sandy was taken to him.

When the nurse wheeled Sandy into the recovery room she saw that O'Neil was already there.

"Oh Sandy." O'Neil said. He did not expect to see her so soon. "How is your foot?"

"I'll be okay but I can't walk for a while." she advised O'Neil.

"Babe." Dan was barely able to speak.

"Yes Baby." Sandy answered as she wheeled her wheelchair beside the gurney where Dan lay. "I'm right here."

"You okay?" "I'm fine and the doctor said that you'll be okay too."

"Dan? This is O'Neil. Can you hear me?"

"Yes Sir."

"Do you know who did this?"

"No idea." Dan told him. "But when you find out I'll be wanting to know."

"Now Dan. You know I can't tell you that."

"You will one way or another." Dan said. "I have two people to recover."

"Well ... they did leave three of their people behind for dead." O'Neil advised. "One of them is still alive."

"Where is he?"

"You're in no shape to do anything anyway so why do you want to know?"

"Where ... is ... he?" Dan said through his grinding teeth.

O'Neil thought for a moment and said. "He's in a room in this hospital under guard by two of my men." O'Neil told him. "Now with that said ... if he accidentally dies from ... oh lets say laying in bed ... and my men are harmed ... I'll be coming for you."

"Yeah I know." Dan said not wanting to say anything else. Then he pretended to pass out but he was wide awake.

"You can talk to him in a day or so." Sandy said. "He'll be feeling a little better then."

"I have a lot of looking around to do at your home." O'Neil told Sandy. "I'll get back to him in a days or so."

"Forgive Dan O'Neil." Sandy told him. "He loves that little girl."

O'Neil smiled. "So do I."

When O'Neil left Dan asked Sandy for his cell phone. He punched a couple of buttons on his phone and then put it to his ear.

"Davis. This is Briks. I need you to get up here to the hospital now. I need to talk to you." He listened as Davis told him a few things and then said; "Just do what you think is best."

Dan handed his phone back to Sandy. He did not look at her knowing that she was eyeballing him.

"You don't call Davis unless you're about to do something secret."

"He's going to be doing something … a few things that I can't do right now."

Sandy knew that calling Davis meant that Dan would be getting secretive and will probably not tell her what was going on.

Almost an hour later Davis walked into the recovery room. Dan was being moved to a private room so Davis waited until he was in the private room and settled down. When the nurse left the room she closed the door.

"How are you doing Sir?" Davis asked as he shook Dan's hand.

"I'm okay but I need to ask you to do a few things. I will be out of commission for a while."

"Yes Sir. What do you need?"

"First … one of the men that attacked us is in a room in this hospital but he is under police guard. Find a way to get into his room and find out where they took Evie and Mary Ann. Then when you find out kill him."

"And what about the police?"

"Try not to harm them but … do what you have to do and then get out of there."

"And the other thing you needed?" Davis asked.

"Get back to me and let me know what you learned. Then we will plan our next move."

"Yes Sir." Davis said. Then he gave Sandy a hug and left the room.

"Dan relaxed. "He'll take care of it. He always does." he said and then fell asleep.

Sandy looked at her husband. She loved him so much and was so proud of him. However; this time he was going against the local police and she did not want him to go to prison. Their baby was due in five months.

Chapter 6

The Ransom

Davis went back to the home. He saw O'Neil walking around but avoided him. He went to what he called his locker of magic and unlocked it. After rummaging around for a few moments he pulled out a small plastic folded case. In it was a gold FBI badge and ID. After changing into a nice suit he left to visit the man in the hospital.

Davis acted just like an FBI agent in every way. This was why Dan used him for things like this. He was very good at what he did. He walked into the hospital and flashed his badge at the woman behind the front desk.

"I need to see a man that was brought in here. He is part of a gang and has two police officers watching him."

"Oh … you're talking about the man in room 101 right down the hall." the woman said.

"Thank you ma'am." Davis said and left for the room.

Davis walked up to the door with two police officers standing outside. He flashed his FBI badge. "I'm Agent Paul Morrie of the FBI. I need to talk to the man in this room.

"Yes Sir." the two officers replied as one opened the door.

When Davis walked in the room one of the officers fallowed him. "I need privacy officer. The questions I will be asking him are not for your ears."

"I'm sorry Sir but we have orders. No one … not even the doctor comes in here without one of us."

"And why is that?"

"To make sure that you do not get hurt."

"Don't you think that I can take care of myself. I have been trained in ways that you cannot even imagine." Davis insisted.

"I still have orders Sir." the officer also insisted.

"Do you like being a cop?" Davis asked.

"I love it Sir."

"You still want to be a cop tomorrow?"

The officer thought for a moment and then left the room. Then Davis turned his attention to the man laying in the bed.

The young man in the bed was about seventeen years old. Being thin from not having enough to eat showed that the gang was not doing well.

"What's you name young man?" Davis asked.

"Who are you?" the young man asked.

"I am FBI Agent Paul Morrie. And what is your name?"

The young man was silent and said nothing.

"Young man ... you are in a lot of trouble but if you answer my questions I can promise you government protection and you will be released rather than going to prison."

The young man thought for a moment and then said; "I'm David."

"Good enough. Calling you young man was getting on my nerves." David trying to get a smile from David. "I need to know where your gang took the two ladies."

"If I tell you ... what will happen to me?" David asked.

"We will put you in the Witness Protection Program. That means that we give you a place to live while you wait to testify for us against your friends in the gang."

"They'll kill me for that." David said.

"They wont be able to find you and you will not be going to prison." David replied. "Right now you are facing two counts of kidnapping and that is at least twenty years. If something happens to them then you'll be facing life in prison." Davis smiled and looked right into David's eyes. "And they are going to love a good looking young man like you in prison. You'll be someone's bitch for sure."

For some reason David started talking. He went on and on telling Davis how they raided the home and grabbed the little girl and her mother. He did not remember anything after that because he was shot. However; he did tell Davis their plans to take the girl to Bacho's home and the mother to the home next door. He even gave Davis the address of Bacho's home.

Davis had all he needed. He quickly pulled a dagger from the inside of his jacket. With his left hand over David's mouth he slid the dagger deep into the young man's chest and into his heart. Davis rolled David's body over on his left side to face away from the door. Then he covered the body up to look like he was sleeping.

Davis stepped out of the room and looked at the two officers. "I want to thank you gentlemen for giving me some privacy but the man did not talk much before falling asleep. I'll come back in a couple of hours and try again."

"Yes Sir." both officers acknowledged.

Davis left and walked out to his truck. A nurse came to give the young man a shot for his pain. One of the officers walked in the room with her. When she rolled David over to wake him up for the shot she saw all of the blood and screened. The officer ran out of the room trying to catch up with Davis but he was to late. Davis was gone.

Dan got a phone call from Davis. "The package has been burned. Will see you in about an hour." Davis said and then quickly hung up. Then he drove back to the home and shaved his beard off so he would not look the same. After shaving he changed clothes again and went back to the hospital.

When Davis arrived at the hospital he found police cars all over the place. He drove to a side door and parked there. Then he went into the hospital and straight to Dan's room.

"Hello Sir." Davis said as he walked into the room.

"The package has been burned?"

"Yes Sir but not before learning where Evie and Mary Ann were."

"I am so glad you work for me." Dan said.

Davis told Dan all that he knew including the fact that Richard and two other men went to Austin just for the purpose of telling Bacho about Mary Ann. He even showed Bacho the picture that the old woman took of Mary Ann as a young

Neanderthal.

"And now I don't have the manpower to assault the Texas Syndicate." Dan said. "I've heard of them. They're viscous."

"We may still be able to go get them." Davis suggested. "It would mean leaving no one at the home to protect it."

"Can't be done." Dan insisted. "However I do want you to do something else."

"What's that Sir?"

"Go to Richard's home and kill everyone there but bring Richard to the Compound and chain him to something. Gag him so he can't yell out. The neighbors are not friendly and would call the police."

"Will do Sir."

Dan looked at Davis and asked; "This doesn't bother you?"

"No Sir. It's part of my job."

"But I have never sent you after Americans before."

"They are your enemy." Davis assured him. "Your enemies are my enemies. Besides … I love that little girl too Sir."

"Okay then." Dan told Davis. "Do it."

"Yes Sir." Davis said as he turned and left the room.

Dan relaxed. Everything was going well but he had to think of a way to get Evie and Mary Ann. Then he remembered Davis suggesting another way to help Evie and Mary Ann. He got on his phone and called Davis back.

"This is Dan. What did you mean a moment ago that there was something else we could do but it would mean leaving the home without security?"

"They are just a ruthless gang but we are highly trained mercenaries. They would not stand a chance."

"But you would be outnumbered almost three to one."

"We've been outnumbered worse than that before and still accomplished our goal." Davis was confident.

"Yeah you're right." Dan agreed. Okay then. Plan it but get with me before leaving."

"Yes Sir." Davis replied. "In the mean time I will take care of this other problem."

"Sounds good." Dan said as the doctor walked in. "The doc just came in so I need to go. I'll see you when I can."

"How do you feel Mister Briks?" the doctor asked.

"Got a lot of pain but that is all."

"Well I did pull out two bullets." the doctor said. "They didn't hit anything but they did make a mess. I cleaned it up but you're going to be here a couple of days."

"Doc." Dan said. "I need to get home as quickly as I can. Two people under my care were kidnapped and I need to find them."

"That's right. That man down the hall was part of the kidnapping." the doctor replied. "Did you have anything to do with his murder?"

"Who's murder?" Dan had to pretend to know nothing about it.

"The young man that was part of that gang that kidnapped the woman and child living at you place was murdered."

Dan looked disappointed. "I was wanting to talk to him ... to hopefully find out where they took Evie and Mary Ann.

"You may fool the doctor here but you're not fooling me." a voice a the door said. It was O'Neil.

"I'll be seeing you tomorrow but you need your rest." the doctor continued. "A nurse will give you something in a minute for that pain."

As the doctor left O'Neil came in. "I told you not to do anything."

"I just found out about the man's murder a few seconds ago." Dan replied.

"You pretended to find out a few seconds ago." O'Neil insisted.

"Get the fuck out of my room you son of a whore." Dan yelled causing nurses and doctors to run to the room.

"Now that's no way to talk to a friend." O'Neil commented.

"Friend my ass." Dan yelled.

Dan's doctor asked O'Neil to leave. Just as Dan gave him an ultimatum. "You come to my home and I'll have your ass shot on sight."

61

"If you want to play that game then I'll play." O'Neil said. "I'll be seeing you in a few days with a warrant for your arrest. Then we can talk."

As the doctors and nurses left the room Sandy's doctor came in. "There you are. You weren't in your room."

"Could we get a room together?" Sandy asked her doctor.

"Well not really. I'm sending you home but you cannot be walking on that foot. I'll write you a prescription for a wheelchair."

"We have one at the house." Sandy advised the doctor.

"No problem then. As soon as you sign some papers then you can go home."

"Can I stay here?" Sandy asked.

"I really need you at the home Babe." Dan mentioned. "One of us needs to be there ruining things and I'll be here another two days."

Sandy thought for a moment. "Okay Baby. I know you're right."

Sandy was wheeled out of the room to where paperwork awaited her signature. After signing the papers she found that Dan had called for someone to come get her. One of God's Angels wheeled her out to their truck and helped her in. When she got home she found three armed members of God's Angels standing at the back door with a wheelchair.

Sandy asked to be wheeled into the kitchen. She was almost hurting for a glass of ice tea. When she got her tea she was wheeled into the den where she was helped out of the wheelchair and onto the couch. Just as she turned on the TV she heard a pickup truck drive into the back yard. Mandy; the security that was there helping Sandy readied her M-16. Everyone at the home was jumpy.

A few minutes later two of God's Soldiers drug a man into the kitchen and dropped him on the floor.

"Oh Sandy. Your home." Davis was surprised to see her.

"Is that our neighbor that told that gang about us?" Sandy asked with so much anger in her voice.

"Yes Ma'am." Davis answered.

"Would you bring him to me please?"

"Yes Ma'am." Davis answered again. She may not have been his boss but her husband was and that was enough to do as she asked. She was the head of God's Angels but he was with God's Soldiers.

Davis had the other two men drag Richard over to Sandy. Then he grabbed Richard's hair and pulled back for him to look at Sandy.

"How dare you come into my home and kidnap two of our friends." Sandy said through her teeth. "If I could get up I'd kick your ass."

"We already did that ma'am." one of the men holding Richard up said. He was proud of what he did.

"You sound happy." Sandy said to the men holding Richard as she laughed.

"This is my home too Ma'am. He sent a gang into my home and kidnapped two of my friends." He jerked back hard on Richard's scalp causing him pain. "Anything I can do to hurt this piece of sh …" The man looked at Sandy and said; "I'm sorry ma'am."

"Thank you Mister Davis." Sandy calmly said. "This helped a great deal."

"Your welcome Ma'am." he said. "When I get through with this is there anything I can do for you?"

"No." she said. "Mandy is doing a great job. Besides I think you have some planning to do."

Davis had Richard taken to a small room where he was thrown on a roll-a-way bed. His pants were pulled off and his feet were tied to the corners of the bed leaving his legs spread apart.

"I'm not going to gag you like Dan wanted because you're having a hard time breathing." Davis told Richard. "But if you start yelling I'll use this cattle prod on your balls and give you a reason to yell." He held up a three foot long cattle prod. Then he pushed the button showing the electric ark shooting from one side of the front poles to the other. "Do you understand?"

Richard agreed with big bulging eyes. A guard was left to watch over Richard. Davis handed the cattle prod to the man watching Richard and left. The guard looked at Richard and smiled and pushed the button on the cattle prod. Then the guard sat in a chair and watched Richard.

Davis went into the library where God's Soldiers planned almost all of their missions. He called in a few of the higher ranking people that survived the attack and started planning. They would have to get past the military which would surely try to stop them. About an hour later Davis went back up to see Richard.

As soon as Davis walked into the room he took the cattle prod from the guard there. "Gag him." he ordered the guard. When Richard was gagged Davis pushed the button on the cattle prod causing it to sizzle in the air.

"Now it is your decision on whether or not I stick this to your balls ... And that little thing ... I think you call a dick." he told Richard. "All I want to know is how you got into the city without the military catching you. You want to tell me or should I start cooking parts of your body ... and guess where I'll be starting?"

Richard nodded his head. Davis removed the rag from Richard's mouth.

"First ... are you thirsty?"

"Very." Richard replied.

Davis ordered the guard to get Richard some water. The guard walked across the hall to the restroom and got a paper cup of water and gave it to Richard.

"I could use more." Richard pleaded.

"As soon as we are finished here." Davis told him. "I need to know how you got into Austin without the government stopping you."

Richard told Davis the name of the street that he turned off of Interstate 35 onto but that was the only street name he knew. It was enough. Davis and his people could find their way to Bacho's home from there.

"Thank you Richard. I'll have your water sent up as soon as

64

I get down stairs." Davis left and kept his word. If he needed Richard's cooperation again he wanted the man to trust his word. He ordered one of the security to take a large glass of water up to the prisoner. Richard was so relieved to get it. He was very thirsty. He also knew that if he cooperated with Davis he would get what ever Davis said.

When Davis got back to the library he went through the maps and pulled out one for Austin. Opening it up on the table he found the road that Richard used to leave the interstate on. Then he found Bacho's address and a rout to use. They now had the location of Mary Ann and her mother Evie. Now to plan the actual attack.

Back at Bacho's home Mary Ann was just waking up. She was groggy but Bacho still tried talking to her.

"Can you hear me Mary Ann?" Bacho asked.

"Where am I?" Mary Ann asked. "Where's my mommy?"

"Your mommy is okay." Bacho said trying to help the girl feel better. "You need to understand that we are your friend. We saved you from those trying to hurt you."

Still dazed and half out of it Mary Ann asked; "Who are you?"

"Just remember that we are your friends." Bacho said again. He did not want her to get mad at them. "The men that took your mommy is our enemy and now your enemy as well. We can help you get your mommy back but it might take a little while."

By time Bacho finished talking to Mary Ann he had her convinced that he and his men really were her friend and that another gang had her mother.

"But rest assure that we will get your mother back." he assured her. "Your father was the Neanderthal that we all heard about over ten years ago isn't he?"

"Yes." she said trusting Bacho.

"I used to be president of a Neanderthal club when I was in school. Those clubs were all over the place." He was telling a lie but he was good at it.

"My mom said that there were a lot of people that believed he was a good man." Mary Ann said proud to talk about her father.

"He was a good man and a good ... Neanderthal." Bacho was playing it up with all he had in him. "Look at all of the things he did to help people and then the government kidnapped him ... like that gang did your mom." Bacho turned to a man standing beside him. He whispered; "Hurry up and lock all of the doors. Put a guard at all doors."

Bacho looked at Mary Ann and asked; "Are you hungry or thirsty?"

"I am." she answered.

"Let's go to the kitchen and get something to eat." he told Mary Ann. "But hold my hand and do as I say if any shooting starts." As he lead her to the kitchen he added; "Your window is boarded up so the bad guys that have your mom cannot shoot you. If you notice almost all windows are boarded up. If they can't see you then they can't shoot you."

"Why do they want to shoot me" Mary Ann asked.

Bacho looked sad as he played his part. "I don't know but I do know that they will not hurt your mom."

Mary Ann got a good look at Bacho. "You look like the man that stuck me with that needle."

"That was probably my twin brother. He is the leader of that gang that has your mom." Bacho was smooth and quick with his answers. "He started his own gang and we have been fighting ever since."

One of the women in the gang lay a large bowl in front of Mary Ann and then some cereal and milk. "This is Sue ... my girlfriend." Bacho introduced her to Mary Ann.

"I am so proud to meet you Mary Ann." Sue said also pretending to be her friend. "Bacho has told me so much about you and your father. Don't worry about your mom. Bacho will get her back."

Sue sat at the table and talked to Mary Ann as Bacho left for a minute to check on a few things. By time Bacho returned Sue had Mary Ann were laughing. That was when Bacho knew that he had everything under control.

"Mary Ann." Bacho said. "I need you to stay here with Sue until I get back. I need to check my men and make sure that the area around this home is secure. I don't need my brother coming in and hurting you. Can you do that?"

"Yes Sir. I like her anyway." Mary Ann said.

As Bacho left he felt good about Mary Ann calling him sir. That told him that everything was going as planned. He walked over to the home next door where Evie was. As he walked into the room where Evie was chained to the bed she looked hard at him.

"Where's my daughter?" she asked.

"Keep one thing in mind ... Evie is it?" Dan said. "If you yell out at anytime you will be gagged. It will be hard to eat with a dirty rag in your mouth. Now can you do that for me?"

"I can do that." Evie agreed. "Now where's my daughter?"

"Your daughter ... Mary Ann is fine but she's about a mile from here."

"Who are you?" Evie asked.

"My name is Bacho but I need to tell you a few things. Then you can ask all you want and I will try to give you the answers. Okay?"

"Do I have a choice?"

"Not really." Bacho said with a grin. "You see this man putting up a cameras?" Bacho pointed at a man at the end of the bed Evie was on.

"So ... what."

"I will say a few things on the camera and you will stay quiet. Then I am going to film you and what happens to you and your little girl depends on what you say. I will ask you questions and you simply answer them on camera. It's that simple. Will you do as I ask?"

"Of course I will."

The man behind the camera turned the camera towards Bacho. Then he turned the camera on and started filming.

"I am Bacho and we have your Evie and Mary Ann." he said

into the camera. "You will pay one million dollars in cash … large bills … and I will give them back to you." Bacho waved for the camera to be turned towards Evie. "This is Evie … as you know. You can see that she is not harmed. Evie … have we harmed you?"

"Not yet."

"Have we fed and given you water?"

"So far."

"She is so testy for some reason." Bacho joked into the camera.

"Now lets get serious. You found this tape in your mailbox. In two days I will check your mailbox. You get your mail around nine in the morning so do not put the box of money in your mailbox until after that. We don't need the mail lady getting your money. If I do not get it you will never see Evie and Mary Ann again. Evie is going to give me your phone number but don't try tracing it. I'll call you in a couple of days to make sure things are going well. And by the way. Mary Ann is doing better than her mom. She's having fun with my girlfriend. Later Dude."

Bacho slid his hand across his throat telling the man to stop filming. The tape was put in a manila envelope and one of his men took it to Dan's home. During the night the man slid the envelope in Dan's oversized mailbox and drove away. Now it was a matter of waiting until the next morning.

Chapter 7

Hot Tempers

Sandy was up early the next morning. As she sat at the kitchen table drinking her coffee one of the security brought the mail to her. "Did you check this package for explosives?" she asked.

"Yes Ma'am."

Sandy looked at Mandy and suggested; "Mandy … get a cup of coffee and sit with me."

Mandy got her cup of coffee and sat at the table close to Sandy.

"Relax Mandy." Sandy suggested again. "Nothing is going to happen now. They got what they came for and there is no reason to comeback."

Sandy opened the package and looked at the tape. Then she pulled out the note and read it.

> *If you want to see Evie and*
> *Mary Ann again you will watch*
> *the tape.*

Sandy asked Mandy to wheel her over to the TV. Once there she handed Mandy the tape and asked her to put it in the VCR. The two women watched the tape. By time it was over the den was almost full of others. Sandy quickly called Dan and told him about the tape. He advised her to do as they wanted. One million dollars was just a drop in the bucket to him.

Sandy called the bank and cleared one it for Sergeant Bensy to pick up the money. The bank had a problem with a stranger coming to get the money but when Sandy told them that she was in a wheelchair and Dan was in the hospital they finally agreed.

Bensy quickly left for the bank.

Dan wanted nothing more than to go home but Sandy was handling things and what could he do that he was not doing from the hospital? However he did ask Sandy to clear it with Davis and send two members of God's Soldiers to him as guards. Things were heating up and he did not need someone walking in and shooting him.

Davis chose two of his men that had CHL's so that they could be armed. They went to the hospital dressed nicely but not wearing their usual camouflaged clothing. Both men stood just inside the room and closely looked over anyone that came in the room.

The hospital called Sergeant O'Neil and complained about the two armed men in Dan's room. O'Neil came to see Dan. When he walked into Dan's room he looked over the two guards.

"They can't be carrying firearms in the hospital Dan." O'Neil suggested.

"They are my bodyguards and they will stay." Dan insisted.

"Couldn't they leave their weapons in their vehicles?" O'Neil asked. "They are big men. They can handle anyone that comes in here."

"They will leave … with their pistols when the doctor releases me."

"I can't allow this Dan." O'Neil suggested. "Even you have to obey the law."

Dan did not like the direction that this was going so he compromised. "I will have them take their pistols out to their vehicles as soon as you put two armed police officers out in the hallway."

"I have a lot going on and my officers are busy." O'Neil said but then thought it over again. "I can give you one officer in the hall but that is all I can do."

Dan thought it over He knew that O'Neil was being worked to death with all that was going on and now a gang has come into his town and kidnapped two people. Dan understood O'Neil's position.

"One officer … 24 hours a day until I leave?" Dan asked.

"I can do that for another day and a half … until you leave." O'Neil agreed.

"When your man gets here then these two will take their weapons out to their vehicles."

"Okay." O'Neil agreed. Then he left leaving Dan more irritated and he was earlier.

About an hour later a police officer walked into Dan's room and told Dan that he was there. Then he drug a chair out into the hallway and sat down for a long day of hard work.

"Okay Guys." Dan said to the two guards in his room. "Take your firearms out to your vehicles and come back. Just leave your pistols. I know you both carry knives but keep them hidden."

"Yes Sir." the two men said as they turned and left the room.

The two men walked out to their vehicles where they were met by the Police department's SWAT team. They were disarmed and arrested for carrying firearms into a hospital. O'Neil went to Dan's room and told him what happened.

"They will be facing only those charges but I warn you to stop." O'Neil told Dan. "Your aggression will not be tolerated."

Release my men or you'll wish you had." Dan warned O'Neil. "You're pushing your weight around and I'll be pushing back."

"What are you going to do Dan?" O'Neil asked smiling in defiance.

"Keep fucking with me you son of a whore." Dan said as he pointed at O'Neil. "I'll have my men walk through you police department and kill everyone wearing a badge. Then we'll takeover the town and you know I have the manpower to do it." Dan lowered his hand. "If you want a war I'll give it to you but you will not survive."

"Threatening me is a felony." O'Neil said as he opened the door and called the officer into the room. "Mister Briks is under arrest for threatening me and the lives of every officer in the department. Treat him as a prisoner."

"Yes Sir." the officer said as he pulled the chair into the room and sat down.

Dan got on his phone and called Davis. He told Davis what happened. Then he gave the order. "Get some of your men here right now … fully armed. We are taking over the town."

The officer quickly slapped the phone out of Dan's hand but the order was already given. He quickly got on his cell phone and called O'Neil telling him what happened.

"Damn it." O'Neil said into his phone. "I really did not think he would do it."

O'Neil quickly drove back to the hospital. Running into Dan's room he yelled; "Stop this now Dan. A lot of innocent people are going to be killed over this."

"When my two men call me and say that they have been released then I will recall the others.

Okay." O'Neil said as he got on his phone and called the police department. "The two men brought in for carrying firearms in the hospital … drop the charges and set them free … quickly."

"If you can hand my phone I'll call off my men."

O'Neil got Dan's phone and handed it to Dan. Dan instantly called Davis and had him hold the others there at the home. Then he added; "If you see anyone … including cops mounting a force on the street kill hem all."

"Break out the explosives Sir?"

"Might be a good idea but keep it all hidden until you absolutely need it." Then he looked at O'Neil and added; "Are you happy now?"

"Yes … I am." O'Neil said. "I'm getting to old for this."

"We can work together on this but I'm doing what I think is best to get Evie and Mary Ann back."

"That's fine." O'Neil said. "My officers will leave your people alone as long as you do not openly break the law. I have a job to do Dan."

"I can do that." Dan agreed. "But when you come out on the Compound you do not look at anything. You will not see anything."

"And I can do that."

"My people will be leaving the Compound in a day or so to go get Evie and Mary Ann. I could use some of your officers for security out there and of course I'll pay them for their time."

O'Neil thought for a moment and said; "I can only give you two. Can you arm them with some of your M-16s?"

"That's no problem but they do not see anything out there either."

"I'll tell them. I do have two officers that were in combat in Afghanistan. I'll send them."

Thanks." Dan said as he stuck out his hand and shook O'Neil's hand.

"Now this is the Dan I used to know." O'Neil said with a smile.

O'Neil stayed there as he and Dan made other plans. As soon as his men got back with Evie and Mary Ann he would lend a few of his people for helping O'Neil. But for now there was a matter of how Davis was doing with his planning.

When O'Neil left Dan called Davis. "Go ahead and stand down. The Sergeant and I made an agreement. We will be working together on some things. Have you heard from the two that were arrested?"

"Yes Sir. They are here right now."

"How are you doing on your planning?" Dan asked.

Everything is ready to go. Just waiting on your word to do it."

Dan thought for a moment and then said; "Do it and good luck."

That evening a man pulled up to Dan's large mail box. Those at the compound watched as the man pulled out the box. It was heavier than it should have been. Two others were in the car with the man. But the box had no money in it but three pounds of C-4 plastic explosive. When the man opened the box it blew up sending parts of the car all over the place. The explosion was so extensive that the bodies of he three men in the car were almost vaporized. What was left burned up in the fire.

Before the police could get there seventeen members of God's

Soldiers and God's Angels drove out of the Compound and headed towards Austin. Their vehicles were loaded down with plenty of extra ammunition and explosives to start a small war. Davis was set on wining this war and anyone that got in their way would be hurt. He did not like hurting anyone in the local police department or in the military but he was going to do his job. Nothing was going to stop them.

As the police arrived at the Compound Sandy walked out to talk with O'Neil. "What happened?" O'Neil asked.

"I guess those in this car were setting an explosive to kill any of us that they could." Sandy replied.

"So your husband did not set up a bomb for them?"

"He wouldn't have done that." Sandy said. "That might kill any neighbors walking or driving by." Then she looked at O'Neil and added; "By the way. Our security is gone. Dan said that you would send two officers to help with security."

"Yes." O'Neil said as he called the two officers over. "This is Sandy." he told the two officers. "She will tell you what she needs."

"Yes Sir." the two officers said as the fallowed Sandy to the kitchen. She needed their names so that they would be paid for their help.

When Bacho had not heard back from the men he sent to collect the money he called Dan. "Where are my men?" he yelled into the phone.

"Who the hell is this?" Dan asked.

"This is Bacho and my men have not called back yet."

"Oh you're the one on the ape." Dan said. "I am in the hospital so my wife is handling it. I know she put the money in the mailbox. She called me after it was there."

"Where are my men?"

"I don't know Bacho." Dan said. "But if you could call back in fifteen minutes I'll calmly wife and have her check the mailbox."

"Okay then. Fifteen minutes." Bacho said and then hung up.

Dan quickly called Davis and told him that Bacho called.

"He's getting very upset."

"We are slowing for our turnoff of the interstate right now Sir." Davis replied. "I'll be talking to Bacho face to face in a few minutes."

"Sounds great." Dan said. "Call me when it's over and wipe out that entire gang."

"I was already planning to do that Sir." Davis said. "Will be calling you soon."

With that Davis hung up. They pulled their vehicles over two blocks from Bacho's home. When his men got out of their vehicles one of Bacho's men cakled in and told him about the military getting ready to attack. He thought that Davis and the others were the military.

Davis and eight of his people would hit Bacho's home and the other nine of them would hit the home where Evie was. They were merciless in their assaults. They fought their way to the bedrooms where Evie and Mary Ann were being held.

As soon as Davis walked into the room where Mary Ann was she yelled; "Mister Davis." Davis took a few moments to tell Mary Ann what was going on.

"You mean they aren't my friends?" she asked Davis.

"No Ma'am." he told her. These are the people that kidnapped you and your mom. The rest of my people are at the home next door getting your mom."

" Mister Bacho told me that she was about a mile from here anthrax another gang leader … his brother … had mom."

"He lied to you." Davis advised her. "Now I don't need you changing into a Neanderthal until we get you and your mom home. If you changed herein front of everyone then the word about you would get out. Do you understand?"

"Yes Sir." she replied.

Davis sent his people down the stairs shooting any gang member they found. Every now and then one of them would set an explosive with a single electric switch to set them all off at one time. As Davis and his people walked out of the home with Mary Ann they met up with the others coming out of the home next door.

Suddenly Mary Ann heard her mom yelling her name. She turned and ran into her mom's arms. Evie scooped up her daughter and continued to run. Once around the corner Davis stopped and handed the controls for the explosives to Mary Ann.

"Now flip the switch." he told her. She flipped the switch. "Now when you push that red button both homes will blow up. Push it when you're ready."

Mary Ann looked at the two building. One was a home where she had made some friends. The other one held her mom and there was no excuse for that. The friends that she made were all lying to her. They were not friends. With a big smile she pushed the red button.

Instantly the explosives in the two homes blew bringing the homes down to the ground. Mary Ann looked at Davis and said; "Thank you. That was fun."

"Lets get you and your mom home and then we can shoot your rifle again."

Mary Ann jumped into the front of Dan's truck and looked out the back window. Then she saw someone that scared her. "Bacho is back there."

"I know." Davis quickly tried to calm her down. "We are taking him back to face your Uncle Dan.

With a big smile Mary Ann said; "Oh he is in so much trouble." Then she turned and sat down leaning against her mom. She slept all the way home as she had, had a trialing few days. But now she was safe in the arms of her mother and surrounded by a few vehicles full of real friends.

Just before getting to the interstate four Humvees pulled out in front of them. Two of them had mounted 50 caliber gins in them. Davis ordered his people to remain in their vehicles. Then he got out to talk to the soldiers that were walking towards them.

"Howdy Lieutenant." Davis said as he stuck out his hand. As the two men shook hands Davis said; I'm Captain Davis of God's Soldiers. We just got back from getting back two of our kidnapped people but we're going home now."

"You'll leave when I say you can." the mouthy lieutenant said.

"Listen Son." Davis said just in time to get yelled at.

"I'm not your son." he yelled I am a lieutenant in the United States army."

Davis got mad. "Boy!" he yelled back. "I have enough gun power behind me to wipe you out and half of the US army." Then he got on his hand held radio and ordered everyone out of the vehicles. We are a mercenary group trained far beyond any training you get. I am leaving your city. You can have this shitty city. I don't want it. If any of you men even point a weapon at us we'll stop and gun you all down. Then we'll still go home."

"Okay … calm down Sir." the lieutenant said realizing that his mouth was about to get them all killed. "We heard a lot of explosions back there. Was that you?"

"Yes." Davis calmed down some. "That gang back there kidnapped two oh our friends. We got our friends back and blew up their homes."

"But that's the Texas Syndicate. They're just plane mean."

Davis took the lieutenant back to his truck and showed him the man in the back. "Is this your man?"

"Yes. That's Bacho." the lieutenant said with much excitement. "He's wanted for many crimes."

"Well we are going to take him to our boss but we can bring him back to you tomorrow.' Davis assured the Lieutenant. "We were going to hand him over to the police anyway." Davis knew that Dan was going to probably kill Bacho himself for what he did but he just needed to get out of there with the gang leader.

"Well I was going to be here for at least a week but with Bacho captured we can go into the city now and take it back over." the Lieutenant said.

"Why let anyone know what happened." Davis said. "When we bring him back to you then you can get the credit for taking the city back."

"Yeah! I might get a raise in rank for that."

"You probably will but I have two people that want to get

home."

The Lieutenant ordered the Humvees moved and flagged Davis and his group on. Davis gave a single wave as he drove past the Humvees and onto Interstate 35. Finally heading home everyone rested. Davis gave Dan a call.

"This is Davis Sir. The two packages are safe and will be delivered in a few hours."

"Loose anyone?" Dan asked.

"All of them and none of us Sir. I also have a surprise for you."

"What kind of surprise?"

"Well Sir … it has two legs and used to lead the Texas Syndicate."

"You actually got Bacho?"

"Tied up in the back of my truck. Two of my people are back there with him making sure he does not … fall out."

"Great job Davis. I'm getting out of here tomorrow."

"Good Sir. Looking forward to seeing everyone together again."

"Then it's until tomorrow."

"Yes Sir. See you tomorrow."

Chapter 8

The Shindig

When Davis and the others drove into the driveway of the Compound Sandy had Mandy wheel her to the back door of the home and on the patio. It seemed like forever as she waited for the line of trucks to come around the home but finally they did. First were two of the vehicles of the others and then Davis drove around behind them. As soon as he stopped Evie and Mary Ann jumped out of the truck and ran to Sandy.

"What happened to you?" Evie asked Sandy.

I was shot in the foot the night they attacked the Compound. Dan was shot in the stomach but he is coming home later today." Sandy looked up at two of the men dragging another man out of the back of Davis' truck. "Who is that?"

"Could you drag Bacho over here guys?" Evie asked. When the men had drug the gang leader over to Sandy and dropped him on his hands and knees Evie continued. "Bacho meet Sandy. You shot her in the foot and shot her husband twice in the stomach." Then Evie raised her voice to a blaring yell. "She's pregnant and you still shot her." Evie cleared her throat. "Sandy meet Bacho. He's the one your husband is going to kill ... oh so slowly." After that Evie quickly turned and kicked Bacho in the ribs so hard she probably broke a few ribs.

"So this is the bastard that invaded my home and killed almost thirty of my friends. My husband will be home from the hospital today. Maybe tomorrow he will deal with you." She looked straight into Bacho's eyes. "I would not want to be you tomorrow."

With a wave of Sandy's hand Mandy pulled her wheelchair back away from Bacho. "Thank you Mandy. The stench was getting to me."

Bacho was taken to the same room that Richard was. He was dropped to the floor and chained to the same bed. Bacho started yelling so the security stuck him with the cattle prod. "That's what you will get every time you yell." He looked at another one of the security. "Take his pants off." Bacho started squirming so the cattle pod was used again. After a few more electrical shocks Bacho got the message and allowed his pants to be removed.

"You can't do this to us. We have rights." Richard yelled. A quick jolt of electricity between his legs reminded him not to yell.

"What are you going to do with us?" Bacho asked.

Security started to stick the cattle prod between is legs but Bacho said; "But I didn't yell."

The guard stopped. "He's right ... right?" he asked the person with him.

"No he didn't."

"Then I can't give him a jolt ... of love?"

"I guess not." the other guard said.

"Oh well." the first guard said as he allowed the end of the cattle to drop to Bacho's crotch. Of course he accidentally pushed the button and held it down.

For a good long four seconds the guard accidentally shocked Bacho and then quickly jerked the cattle prod back. Bacho was almost crying from the pain. "I hope Dan lets me kill you for killing my friends."

"You can't keep torturing us this way." Richard yelled. The guard raised the cattle prod. "Oh shit." Richard said just before the electrodes hit him between the legs again.

When the guard raised the cattle prod he handed it to the relieving guard. If they even talk to each other shock'em again. We don't need them planning an escape. If they get away Dan will have our asses."

"No problem."

Sandy called Dan and told him that Evie and Mary Ann were back. He told her that the doctor was releasing him and she needed to come get him. When they hung up he called Davis.

"Yes Sir." Davis said.

"All of you did a great job. Tell them that they will all see a little more on their checks this month."

"Thank you Sir but this is something that we all would have done free."

"I know but you all deserve it." Dan added. "In the meantime have a few of the men run downtown and get three large bar-b-q pits and plenty of bar-b-q sauce. Don't forget the sausage and chicken and anything else you all want ... including the beer."

"Yes Sir."

Get some of that green oak wood from the trees but you will need some hot coals to get it going." Dan suggested.

"Charcoal from the store will get it started." Davis was getting excited.

"Good thinking. The green wood will smoke the meat. Tell the men to bring out any of their girlfriends. We are going to have us a shindig."

"Sir." Davis said. You have a couple of things to take care of upstairs today and getting all of these things would take time. Wouldn't you rather have your ... shindig tomorrow?"

"Again Davis ... good thinking." Dan cleared his throat. I was getting excited. I'll be home in a few hours. I'll call you when I'm on my way."

"Yes Sir." Davis said and then hung up.

Two of God's Angels came to the hospital to get Dan while four others went to get the bar-b-q pits, food and beer. The two that came to get Dan walked into the hospital. O'Neil was walking out when he saw the men from Dan's group. Stopping them he asked if they were carrying firearms.

"But we have CHLs." one of them said.

"But you still cannot carry a firearm in a hospital." O'Neil advised."

"Are we in trouble?"

"Oh what the hell." O'Neil said as he walked off.

Feeling dumbfounded the two men looked at each other and continued onto Dan's room. As they walked into his room they heard Dan yelling at them from behind. He was signing his paperwork.

"Now you need to take it easy Mister Briks." his doctor said as the two men walked up. "And you two need to see that he takes it easy."

The two men laughed. "Like we are going to tell him what to do." one of them commented. He might have to wait a while but … when he is feeling better he'll kick our butts." The men continued to laugh.

"Mister Briks." the doctor said. "If you do not take it easy then you could find yourself back in here. You really need to stay in here another few days but … if you take it easy …"

"I know Doctor." Dan explained. "I'll go home and straight to bed." I'll stay in bed for a good two days and even then only get up if I'm feeling better."

"I know you Dan." the doctor said. "You're my friend and I worry about you. You're still hurt bad and if you do not get your rest something could go wrong inside your stomach and you could die. Then what good will you be to anyone?"

"I'm sorry Doc." Dan said. I promise to take it easy but we are having a big bar-b-q tomorrow. Please bring the wife and enjoy yourselves."

"We might do that. By the way. The other four of your people were released yesterday. They were not hurt as badly as you."

After all of the papers had been signed the two men took Dan out to the truck. One helped him in and the other got in the driver's seat to drive back. When the second one was in the truck they left for the Compound. On the way home they had to stop by the pharmacy to get another wheelchair. Sandy was using the only one they had at the Compound.

When Dan's pick-up drove around the back of the house everyone there went to meet him. Mandy wheeled Sandy right up to the truck. When he was helped out he tried to bend over to kiss Sandy. She strained to stand but even with others helping her she barely got high enough for a quick peck on the lips.

"That's okay Baby." Sandy said. "I'll get you when you're in the bed." Everyone ooooooed at what she said.

Dan was taken to his bed and helped into it. Sandy had to go around to the right side of the bed and climb in beside her man. Mary Ann was had pulled up a chair on his left side and sat in it. She was not moving.

"Wow!" Dan said. "I have a beautiful woman on both sides of me."

Mary Ann got up and kissed her Uncle Dan on the cheek and then sat back down. Then she told everyone; "You hear that. I'm beautiful." Of course everyone laughed at that one.

"I'm sorry everyone but I have some business to tend to." Dan told everyone. "However; any of you that want to stay may since what these two men did effected us all."

"Mister Briks." one of the security said. "Sergeant O'Neil is downstairs to see you."

Dan thought for a moment and then said to bring him up. Seconds later O'Neil walked in and smiled.

"I was hoping you would let me come up and see you." O'Neil said as he reached out and shook Dan's hand. "How are you feeling?"

"I'll be okay after a few years." Dan said with a big smile.

"I'm sorry I went as far as I did but I had a job to do." O'Neil said.

"That's okay my friend. Like you said ... you had a job to do." Dan said. "I'm sorry for pushing back so hard but ... I had a job to do too."

"Do all of your people have CHLs" O'Neil asked.

"All but one of them do."

Then they can open carry their pistols only in town. No other weapons though. This show of force might stop anyone else ... another gang from coming into our little town. I'll talk to the Sheriff about us asking everyone with a CHL to open carry if they wish.

"I don't think he'll go for that. He's a bleeding heart liberal communist." Dan advised.

"Yeah but I am running for Sherriff so help me to get elected and I …" He stopped abruptly.

"You what?" Sandy asked.

"I was going to promise a few things but let me make sure I can do them first." Everyone in the room laughed.

"Well … my friend … I am about to dispense some of my justice." Dan advised O'Neil. "Is my friend here beside me or is a cop beside me?"

O'Neil thought for a moment and said' I would like to see how you handle problems so … a friend stands beside you."

Bring in Bacho." Dan ordered. A minute later Bacho was forced to the floor a few feet from Dan's bed.

"Bacho. Do you know me?"

"No." Bacho said.

"Well you should. You shot me in the stomach twice."

Bacho looked up. "You're Dan Briks but some of my men shot you."

"Yes I am Dan Briks." Dan said as others in the room laughed.

"Do you know why you're here?"

"You're gon'a kill me?"

"Yes I am. Well actually thanks to you shooting me … one of my people will kill you."

"Please have mercy on me. I'm sorry." Bacho pleaded for his life.

Suddenly Mary Ann jumped up and kicked Bacho in the face. "You stuck a needle in me and then hurt my mom." She started to change as she continued to yell at the now crying man. "Your gang killed many of my friends. Now I …"

"No Mary Ann." Evie quickly stopped her. Mary Ann ran to her mom crying. "I just want to kill him" she said as she changed back into that lovable little girl.

"Do you see what you have done to this little girl?" Dan asked as his rage almost exploded. "Davis." he yelled. "Take this man into the woods in the back yard …" he looked at Mary Ann. And with Evie's permission take Mary Ann with you. When you get to the woods let her do what ever you want to him."

Evie was not sure if she wanted her little girl to kill a man but she had already killed one man. What was another. She knew that her daughter had to vent the anger she had so with a smile she said; "Go with the men if you want to Baby."

With her face half changed back to a Neanderthal she walked past her mom. "Thank you Mommy."

"Now bring Richard in here." Dan ordered.

When the four men got back to the trees with Bacho and Mary Ann they let Bacho hit the ground hard. His feet were tied to a tree so he could not run. By this time Mary Ann was full Neanderthal. When Bacho looked up and saw the young Neanderthal he screamed. "No. Don't let her touch me."

The young Neanderthal growled and showed her teeth. Then she slowly raised her hands towards Bacho. As she slowly closed her hands together Bacho started screaming from pain. When his head imploded and the others around her realized what she was doing. With blood and brains all around the man; Bacho was dead.

"We'll come back and clean up the mess later." one of the security said.

As they turned to walk back to the house they saw that O'Neil was there.

"I had no idea that you could do that." O'Neil told Mary Ann.

"He won't hurt me or my mom again." she told O'Neil as she walked past him.

"I guess he won't will he." O'Neil whispered to himself.

O'Neil fallowed Mary Ann and the four guards back upstairs to Dan's room. Dan was still yelling at Richard but stopped when he saw Mary Ann walking in.

"You okay Mary Ann?" Dan asked her.

"I killed him. He'll never hurt anyone again." she said as she hugged her Uncle Dan.

"But are you okay?" he asked her again.

Mary Ann thought for a moment and then said; "I'm okay

I guess."

"Just sit beside me or you can go play if you want." Dan suggested.

"Is this the neighbor that brought those bad men here." Mary Ann asked.

Yes but let me take care of this one." Dan advised. "You can't have all of the fun."

Mary Ann looked at Dan and smiled. "I'll let you take care of this one."

Dan looked at O'Neil and asked; "You still with us?"

"I'm still here and learning a lot." O'Neil said as he swallowed the lump in his throat. It was like watching the mafia executing people but he did like the way Dan handled things. *With elections coming up maybe this man should run for judge.* O'Neil thought to himself.

"Now back to you Richard." Dan said. "What should I do with you?"

"I have one question if you don't mind." O'Neil said. "Why were both men in here in front of this girl with no pants on?"

"We were trying to get some information from them." Dan said. "So when they would not answer or they started yelling we did this." he said as he waved and the man with the cattle prod.

"No, no." Richard yelled. As soon as the cattle prod touched Richard between the legs he started screaming. For four long seconds Richard was being shocked until Dan waved the cattle prod away.

"That's why he wasn't wearing pants."

"Now back to you Richard." Dan said again. "What should I do with you?"

"Just don't use that thing again." Richard begged.

"Well ... I am going to kill you but how should I do it? You went all the way to Austin to find someone to attack us. Then they killed almost thirty of my people and shot me twice. He raised his voice and yelled; "And you shot my wife and she is pregnant."

Dan hurt himself with that one and had to lay back down.

Sandy rolled her wheelchair closer to her husband and put her arm around him. "Can we finish this tomorrow Baby?"

"No." he said. "We have to finish this now. We have the party tomorrow." As Dan breathed heavily he ordered Davis to take Richard out to the trees and kill him. "Make sure he suffers a little bit first."

"Yes Sir." Davis said as he and three others drug Richard out of the room screaming.

A few minutes later a shot was heard and then a second one was heard coming from the tree line. Then there were two more shots. Finally there was a fifth shot. By time Davis came back up to Dan's room everyone had left except O'Neil.

"He's … gone Sir." Davis said.

"Why did I hear five shots?" Dan asked.

"I think the sights on my pistol are off a bit." Davis said. "At first I shot at his head but hit both of his kneecaps. Then I aimed higher and fired two time but hit his left and right hip. Then I aimed real high and put the last bullet in his head."

"You need to set those sights." Dan advised.

"I'll go out to the woods tomorrow and do that Sir."

"Good man." Sandy came in and gave Dan a strong pain pill that would help him sleep. "I've been meaning to ask you something Babe. How are you getting upstairs with the wheelchair?"

"Oh I just tell one of the men that I need to get upstairs and they carry me up. Then they go back and get the wheelchair, help me into it and I come in here."

The men finally came back with the things for the party. They got three large bar-b-q pits and a small standup cooler. They set up the cooler close to the back door where there was an outside electrical plug. Then they filled it with the meat. The beer went into garbage cans and were filled with ice. The next morning they would go back into town for more ice as this ice would melt during the night.

Around nine in the morning everyone started gathering in the back yard. It was a bit cool that morning so those helping

Dan and Sandy made sure they wore their coats. Then they were taken downstairs and wheeled outside and under one of the trees to one side of the back yard.

The bar-b-q pits were already going and meat was cooking. On the pits was sausage links, chicken halves, pork chops, and some boudan. Some vegetables were also smoked like corn on the cob, onion halves, and potato halves. Two gallons of potato salad and macaroni salad topped off the meal.

At noon Dan called everyone's attention and opened the party in prayer.

"Father we come to you in the name of your son Jesus Christ. Thank you for bringing us all here this day. We not only celebrate getting Evie and Mary Ann back but we celebrate the help you gave us in doing it. We lost not one person Lord and I thank you for that. But Lord … I need to rebuild my ranks. Please send me the people I need. I also thank you for all the food we have here today and ask that you bless it and make it nourishment unto our bodies. Amen.

Someone yelled; "And thank you Lord for the beer too." Others cheered.

"Now dig in." Dan yelled as he laughed at the beer comment. "This is your day … your party … so have fun."

Dan and Sandy were wheeled over to a table that had the cooked meat in different large pans. Dan loved his boudan and got three links. A little potato salad and macaroni salad and he was ready to eat. When their plates were full they were wheeled to a folding table where Dan started making a pig of himself. Sandy on the other hand was very much a lady. While Dan ate his boudan with his hands Sandy cut hers with a knife and ate it with a fork.

Evie was also a lady and ate her pork chops using a knife and fork. But when it got down to the meat that was left on the bone it was all hands. Mary Ann loved her bar-b-qed chicken. The sauce on her hands and face told everyone how she ate her chicken.

The others were having fun as well. This was something that Dan had never done before but thought about doing it every now and then; maybe once every three months or after all missions.

The party lasted far into the night but when the beer ran out the party was over. The left over meat and salads were put in the cooler. Anyone could come get what they wanted during the night. One of the pans full of meat was taken to the barracks and placed in their large refrigerator.

Three of the men got drunk but they kept their composure. One of them walked around with one of the gallon tubs of the macaroni salad. With a large wooden kitchen spoon in hand he ate the whole thing before passing out around midnight.

Mary Ann fell asleep in her mom's arms that night. She thought that she had lost her mom. A smile was on her face as she slept. She dreamt of finding her father and him holding her. Then she woke up. Remembering her dream she started crying.

Chapter 9

The Restaurant

Dan had hurt himself when he yelled at Richard. Then he ate to much at the party. The combination of the two things was causing him more pain. Finally he had two of the security take him back to his doctor.

"Well Dan ... I told you to take it easy." the doctor said.

"I know Doc." Dan agreed. "But the food was so good. You missed a great party."

"There was an emergency here at the hospital and I was needed."

"Maybe you can make the next one." Dan suggested.

"Dan ..." the doctor said. "I'm putting you backing the hospital for a few days. I need to watch your abdomen and make sure you haven't messed things up in there."

"Yes Sir." Dan said as depression set in. He did not like hospitals but asked one of the two guards with him to go get a crossword puzzle book. Dan loved his crossword puzzles.

Dan called Sandy and told her that he would be back in the hospital a few more days. "Yeah ... he wants to watch my stomach a few days to make sure I'll be okay."

"I told you to take it easy." Sandy argued.

Dan rolled his eyes and let out a heavy sigh. "Yes dear." Every time she said something else he answered with a calm; "Yes dear.

"Are you listening to me?" she nagged again.

"Yes dear."

"If you don't heal properly you'll be no use to anyone." she advised.

"Yes dear."

Sandy realized that she was driving Dan crazy and stopped

her nagging." I love you Baby and I need you home."

"I'll do what the doctor said and I should be home in a few days." Dan advised her. "And I love you too Babe."

"Don't worry about things here. I'll take care of everything." Sandy assured her husband.

"I know you will." Dan said. "You always do."

With the local threats out of the way it was a time for healing. Most of those that died at the Compound had no families and were buried at the back of the back yard where Mary Ann had destroyed so many trees. Thirteen graves were a testimony to what others could do to them. They were also a reminder to what revenge looked like.

As Dan lay in his hospital bed O'Neil walked in. "Ha boy."

"The only boy here is between your legs." Dan replied. "Am I in trouble ... again?"

"No but I would like to throw an idea at you." O'Neil said.

"Okay then. What is it?"

"You know I am running for Sherriff right?"

"Yes." Dan said as he wondered what his friend was getting at.

"How would you like to be a judge?" O'Neil asked. "If I were the Sherriff and you were the Judge ... can you imagine what we could do to stop these gangs and terrorist around here?"

Dan thought about what O'Neil said. "But I don't know the laws much."

"Not many of them do." O'Neil replied. "They mostly use their powers to push a liberal communist agenda. They decide what laws to fallow and what laws not to fallow. We can push a Conservative Republican agenda. We could make this town safer for those that live here. What liberal will do that?"

"Let me think about it." Dan suggested. "I'll also need to talk to Sandy and God about this."

"No problem." O'Neil said. "I've got to go and play policeman."

As O'Neil left the room Sandy walked in with help from Mandy. "Ha there." Sandy said. She and O'Neil talked for a moment and then he left.

Three days later Dan was out of the hospital handpicking his bed.

"What are you doing?" Dan asked Sandy who was upstairs without her wheelchair.

"Oh hush." Sandy insisted. "Even with me walking on it, it hardly hurts. Besides; Mandy is helping me."

Dan let out a heavy sigh. He was happy to see her waking again but it still bothered him. "If you're walking then I want to come downstairs."

Mandy went downstairs and got two of the men to help Dan downstairs. Once he was downstairs he went straight to the kitchen and had one of the men get him a cup of coffee. As he sat at the kitchen table Davis came up and sat with him.

"I overheard you and O'Neil talking about you running for County Judge."

"Well … a Judge position."

"The lowest Judge position is County Judge."

"Then maybe I'll run for County Judge."

"It's going to cost you a lot of money in campaign signs and flyers."

"I know." Dan replied sadly. "That is the downside."

"On the other hand … I think his idea is a good one."

Sandy came to the table and sat down with her own cup of coffee. "What'cha two talking about?"

"I'm thinking about running for County Judge." Dan told her.

"I thought O'Neil was joking about that."

"Nope. And neither am I." He looked at Davis. "I'll do it."

"Are you crazy old man?" Sandy asked.

"Yes but; only from the shoulders up."

Sandy looked at Davis who was laughing. "What are you laughing about?"

"Nothing Ma'am." he said as he got up and left the kitchen; still laughing.

"If you become a Judge you'll be on every hit list in Texas."

Every gang member not to mention Allah's Right Hand will be looking for you."

"You're right." Dan replied. "I need to get more contracts for God's Soldiers and get some money coming in here." Dan said out loud as he thought.

"Oh … he's not listening to me again." Sandy yelled as she walked out of the kitchen with Mandy running to catch up with her.

When Sandy was gone Davis felt that it was safe to come back to the kitchen. When he sat down beside Dan he was still smiling.

"Yeah you had better watch that." Dan suggested with a smile. "She'll get you."

Dan and Davis spent the next hour drinking coffee and planning his strategy for running for County Judge.

Ever since the word went out that God's Soldiers was looking for a few good men and women phone calls had been coming in from all around. Dan was excepting applications from anyone with prier military experience and a honorable discharge. However; with him running for County Judge Dan left the training of the new applicants to Davis.

One of these new applicants was Robert Moes, a cousin to Davis. Robert had just got out of the Marines with a long list of medals and a long list of disciplinary actions as well. He was a hero in many ways but he had a problem with authority. He liked doing things his way rather than doing things the way he was told to do them.

Davis knew that his cousin could be a problem but God's Soldiers needed to be rebuilt. He knew that Dan needed the money from missions to pay for his campaign for Judge.

The new applicants had to go through a three month training period. The training camp was being built in the back yard close to the tree line and into the trees. Dan did not use outside contractors to build his training camp but used his own people. He already had the barracks where the new applicants would sleep so building the rifle range, obstacle course, and other things need was simple. It did not take a professional carpenter to build any of it.

Within two weeks Dan had twenty seven applicants. Maybe ten to fifteen would finish and become members of God's Soldiers. After a period of time some of them would work their way into God's Angels.

Dan no longer worried about the military looking for Mary Ann after Allah's Right Hand had taken over Fort Hood and other military facilities. What he did not know was that the military had taken back almost all of their facilities and bases. Fort Hood was one of the bases taken back.

Although the United States government no longer cared about Mary Ann, Major Frank Gillis did. The building in which he operated his assault against Evie and Mary Ann was not touched by the terrorist that had taken the base. He got all of the personnel employees back and was working on getting the Satellite Room rebuilt. With Michael being captured there was no one with a chip in them to fallow but he might need the Satellite Room later. He could still use the satellite to track someone once he located them.

When Major Gillis called his team back to work he also called Sergeant Bails back as well. Bails had not talked to Dan in quite a while but now that he was back to work for the Major he started learning what was going on. One Saturday morning he drove to the Compound to talk with Dan.

Sandy was walking around much better when on a Saturday morning she answered the front door. "Well howdy Bails." she said as she gave him a hug. The others are in the kitchen."

Sandy lead Bails into the kitchen where Evie and Dan sat at the kitchen table. They were both happy to see the Sergeant.

"Our prodigal son has come home." Dan said as he stuck out his hand. "So what brings you out here today?"

"It's Major Gillis again." Bails said. "He's putting things back together again to start tracking someone."

At that time Mary Ann skipped into the kitchen. "Sergeant Bails." she said surprised to see him.

Mary Ann gave Bails a hug and then sat at the table. Evie got up and got him a cup of coffee and sat it in front of him as she sat back down at the table.

"You all have problems coming from Major Gillis again." Bails warned then all. "He's back to building up that building and the Satellite Room."

"But no one here has one of those chips in them so why should we worry?" Evie asked.

"The chip … like that one that was in Michael was only used to locate him." Bails advised them. "Once they found him they just fallowed him where ever he went from the satellite."

"So why should we worry about that?" Sandy asked.

"If they find little Mary Ann here then they can fallow her around." Dan advised them all.

"And that satellite can look right into this home and find her too." Bails said. "Of course they are not going to look into every home in the country but if they have an idea where she might be then they might look into all of the homes in that area."

"I wonder if Richard told anyone else about Mary Ann … someone that might tell Gillis." Evie wondered.

"Well … there's no way of knowing now that he's dead." Dan said.

The four talked for a while before Bails said that he had to head back. Dan felt safe that Major Gillis had no idea as to where Mary Ann was but they had to keep her on the Compound for sure now. Dan would also make sure that Davis kept the trainees on alert and ready to fight at any time.

Davis had been training the new members of God's Soldiers. A few had dropped out and a few more were sent home. None of them knew about Mary Ann and what she could change into. Once they were chosen for God's Soldiers then they would know only that she was like her father. Any of them that were chosen for God's Angels knew more about her because they were chosen to protect her and her mom Evie.

With Dan and Sandy's baby due in just three months Sandy was busy setting up a place in their bedroom for the baby. The doctor was going to tell them if the baby was a boy of girl but they did not want to know. However; this made it hard to buy things like blue or pink sheets, blankets, baby book, and so on. Finally one day when they were visiting the doctor they asked him to tell them. Dan and sandy were about to have little boy.

While Sandy started buying blue things for the bedroom which they would share with the baby, Dan went out and bought a Ruger 10/22 rifle. The baby was not even born yet and Dan was already buying guns for him. Now that they knew that the baby was going to be a boy everyone was getting excited.

Mary Ann was also getting excited. In three months she would have a new baby to take care of. She could only do so much with her doll. But Sandy had other plans for her son.

One evening they all went out to eat at a local bar-b-q restaurant. Mary Ann was warned to be on her best behavior. For no reason was she to even change a little. She understood this and gave her word to do nothing as far as changing into the young Neanderthal girl they all loved.

Dan, Sandy, Evie, and Mary Ann sat at a large table in the corner of the dining room of the restaurant. The adults got a glass office tea while Mary Ann got her favorite; root beer.

This restaurant had a large buffet with every kind of Tex-Mex food a person might want. As the four got up and got what they wanted they noticed a man yelling at his wife. Everyone in the restaurant noticed him.

Dan and the others sat at their table and waited for Mary Ann. She was a little slower than the others but she insisted on getting her own plate of food. At age ten she was a big girl now.

The man at the table in another corner of the restaurant continued to yell at his wife. Then suddenly he slapped her.

"Just pay no attention." Dan said as he stood and walked over to the man.

The man looked up at Dan and asked; "What the hell do you want?"

"I'm gon'a have to ask you to watch your language. We have a child over there." He turned and pointed at Mary Ann. When he turned back to face the man he found the man already standing just inches in front of him.

Suddenly the man swung his elbow against Dan's face knocking him to the floor. Dan was out cold. Sandy and Evie ran to Dan's side but no one was watching Mary Ann.

The man sat back down as he laughed at Sandy and Evie trying to pull Dan away. Then he looked up and saw Mary Ann standing there looking at him. She was very angry and her face showed it.

"What are you looking at … you little bitch?" the man yelled at Mary Ann.

"You're a bad man and I hate you." Mary Ann told the man.

"No little girl." the man's wife said trying to warn Mary Ann.

The man stood and took one step towards Mary Ann. "Who do you think you are?"

"My name is Death … and I have come for you." Mary Ann quickly changed into the young Neanderthal girl and raised her hand towards the man.

"What the hell." the man said as he looked puzzled.

Suddenly Mary Ann let out an ear piercing scream that shook the restaurant and caused the dust to fall from the rafters in the ceiling. Then she plunged her hands forward towards the man as an invisible force picked him up and forced him through the brick wall to the outside of the building. Then the man began to rise off of the ground but not from his doing. The ground and the restaurant began to shake harder. Then suddenly the man's body tore apart in numerous pieces. The ground stopped shaking and Mary Ann returned to being the little girl that those with her loved.

By this time Dan was up but still half out of it. He had enough composure to have Sandy and Evie get Mary Ann out to the truck. He climbed into the passenger side while Sandy got behind the wheel. Sandy cranked up the motor to the truck and left the parking lot with dust and gravel flying all around.

A few minutes later the truck fly around the home and to the back door. Dan got out allowing Evie and Mary Ann out. The four wasted no time getting into the home.

Dan quickly called Davis and told him what happened. Davis would have to step up security in case any of the town's people came out. It would be worse if the dead man's family came out. What Dan did not know was that the man that Mary Ann killed had four brothers. The dead man's name was David Boren.

The Boren family had been feared for many years. When their father and mother died in a car wreck the boys had to raise themselves. They grew into large men and pushed their way around to get what they wanted. All five of them had been arrested many times. When the four Boren brothers learned of their brother's death they went on a rampage.

By that night they had gone to the bar-b-q restaurant and chased out any of the customers that were there. Then they beat up the restaurant manager because he would not tell them who killed their brother. He did not know who Mary Ann and the others were but told them a story of a child; a little girl that changed into a monster and killed their brother. The Boren brothers did not believe the manager's story and left him barely alive on the restaurant floor. Before leaving they warned him that if he called the cops they would come back and he would not survive the next visit. Luckily for him a few of the customers called the cops. Just minutes after the Boren brothers left the police and an ambulance was at the restaurant.

"I can't tell you who did this Sergeant." the manager told O'Neil. "They said that if I turned them in they would come back and kill me."

"They hum." O'Neil said. "You're talking about the Boren brothers."

"No, no." the manager insisted. "It wasn't them.

"So David Boren was killed here tonight and his brothers did not come to find out who killed him." O'Neil said. "Is that what you're trying to get me to believe?"

The manager was almost crying. "If you go out there they'll kill me."

"If they did this then I would take every police officer I had

98

out there to get them all." O'Neil said. "I just need you to tell me if they did this."

The manager finally admitted to O'Neil that the four Boren brothers were there and that all four of them beat him up. The manager was so scared that he was shaking. With the restaurant needing repairs he decided to close for the repairs. He would spend most of his time at home. O'Neil assured the manager that he would not go after the four brothers until the next day. He had more things to investigate; people to see and talk to.

O'Neil left the restaurant and drove out to the Compound. He kept it professional and parked close to the front door. As he walked up to the front door and got ready to knock the door opened. Dan stood in the doorway holding the door knob.

"I figured you would be here sooner or later." Dan said as he stepped out of the way so O'Neil could come in. The two men walked into the kitchen where Sandy and Evie were and sat down at the table with them. Evie got up and got O'Neil a cup of coffee and then sat back down in her chair.

"I have no doubt in my mind that little Mary Ann was at the bar-b-q restaurant today and that she changed and killed a man." O'Neil told them. "I need to hear your story."

Dan, Sandy, and Evie told O'Neil what they saw and did. O'Neil looked in the back yard and saw Mary Ann playing with her doll.

"Witnesses at the restaurant say that a little girl turned into some kind of monster and killed the man but … that was all they knew. They did see that the man was slapping his wife."

"Yes Mary Ann killed the man but he deserved it." Evie said.

"Well … until I find a monster I cannot make an arrest." O'Neil said. "But she needs to stop showing herself as a Neanderthal child. The public is starting to notice."

"I know." Dan agreed. "I'll start working with her on it again. But if I could have changed into a bigger and younger man I would have killed him too. I tried to step in but I guess I'm getting to old."

"We need to work on keeping it quiet around here about Mary Ann. With me running for Sherriff and you running for County Judge we do not need anyone connecting us to the Neanderthal child."

"I agree." Dan said. "We need to keep it quiet."

Chapter 10

Neanderthal Child

Davis had to go ahead and let the trainees know about Mary Ann but swore them to secrecy. However; his cousin, Robert Moes saw an opportunity to make some money. He was not sure how he could make money off of this new information but he would give it some serious thought.

God's Soldiers were put on full alert. The trainees were also on full alert but continued with their training. One morning Dan sat on the balcony drinking his coffee and watching the trainees run the new obstacle course.

"Good morning Father." Dan prayed. *"I have many irons in the fire right now and I need your help. I am running for County Judge but no one knows me. Please help me with that Father. And now Mary Ann has shown herself as the Neanderthal child again and she killed another man. All of this could ruin my chances of becoming a County Judge. Father ... please watch over all of us and help me to become the County Judge. Thank you for taking time to listen to me. Amen.*

Dan continued sipping on his coffee until the cup was empty. Then he went back to the kitchen downstairs to get another cup. When he got to the kitchen he found Sandy and Evie sitting at the table talking. He refilled his cup with coffee and added the sugar and milk. After a quick stir he got the cup and sat at the table.

"We were just talking about Mary Ann." Evie told Dan. "She has got to stop changing in public."

"I don't think we need to take her into the public's eye for a while." Dan advised.

At that time Mary Ann walked around the corner and pulled

a chair up to the table. After sitting down she played with her doll.

"Mary Ann." Dan said softly.

"Yes Uncle Dan." Mary Ann replied.

"Put your doll down. We need to talk about your changing and killing that man two days ago."

"What now." she said. "He was a bad man."

"I agree Baby Doll but you still need to stop changing in public." her mother said. "You're making things dangerous for all of us around here."

"What do you mean dangerous?" Mary Ann asked.

"Every time you change in public more and more people see you as ... what some are calling ... the Neanderthal child." Dan advised her. "Sooner or later someone is going to see you out here and then all our lives will be in danger."

"But that man was a bad man." Mary Ann tried to defend herself.

"I agree but you have got to stop changing in public." Dan argued. The government probably already knows that you're around here someplace. You heard Bails. Major Gillis is already rebuilding the Satellite Room so he can track you ... when he finds you. I would not put it past the Major to bomb this home if he cannot get you."

They all agreed to not take Mary Ann into town for a while. Many of those in the restaurant saw Mary Ann as a human child that changed into what they first called a monster. She could not go into town again for a while allowing them time to forget her face. As security increased on the Compound the people in their small Texas town were starting to fear the renegade child that was changing into a monster and killing people.

That morning Evie and Sandy were watching the local news on the TV when pictures were shown of Mary Ann confronting the man at the restaurant. The pictures showed her changing into the Neanderthal child. Sandy started recording the news cast to show Mary Ann what she was causing. Hopefully this might show her the dangers that she was causing them all. When the report was over Evie called Mary Ann into the den.

"Yes Mommy." Mary Ann said as she stepped in front of her mom.

"We need to show you what was on the TV this morning." Sandy said.

Mary Ann backed up to her mom and looked at the TV. Sandy played back the news broadcast. Mary Ann watched and finally realized what her mom and the others were talking about.

"This is why you cannot change in public for any reason." Evie said. "This world is full of bad people but you cannot be killing all of them. You shouldn't be killing anyone anyway."

"So I shouldn't have killed that man?" Mary Ann asked.

"You need to learn to weigh the consequences." Sandy advised her. On one hand the man did deserve to die. On the other hand Major Gillis has probably seen this news broadcast and is looking for you with his satellite right now. Now if he finds you he might send in soldiers to grab you like they did your father. So knowing what could happen ... was it worth changing and attacking that men?"

"Not really." Mary Ann admitted. "So ... no matter what ... I shouldn't stop a man like that."

"You can yell at him all you want. You just should not change. You need to learn when to change and when not to." Sandy advised her.

"And we will talk about that later ... okay?" Dan said.

"Okay Uncle Dan." Mary Ann said as she walked away.

Later that evening Dan got with Mary Ann and had another talk with her. This time he told her that it was best to never change in the public's eye. She should never change unless she could do it without being seen and, if she knew that she could get away without anyone knowing that she was the Neanderthal Child.

Word was getting around town and the county about what everyone was calling the Neanderthal Child. Many wondered if this Neanderthal Child could be related to the Neanderthal heard of ten years earlier. The name "Neanderthal Child" went out

103

over the airways and before long across the country. Within days of the incident at the restaurant Major Gillis saw it on his office TV. Finally he had found the child of the Neanderthal. But, exactly where was she?

Major Gillis knew of the town where the bar-b-q restaurant was so he would start his search there. Gillis made his plans to invade the small town with spies. He sent three men and one woman into the town to rent a home and infiltrate the public as new members of the community.

Mildred, Mark, and Mat were Second Lieutenants while Buford was a First Lieutenant and the one in charge. Mark and Mildred would pretend to be married. They were the ones that rented the home. As soon as Bails found out about the four spies he learned all he could about them and then went to see Dan and the others.

Bails arrived on a Saturday morning as he always had. This time he drove around to the back yard and parked under one of the large oak trees. He did not want Major Gillis to spot his truck with the satellite. By time he stopped his truck he found himself looking down the barrels of four M-16 rifles.

"Stand down." one of the guards yelled out to the others. "He's a friend."

The trainee for God's Soldiers opened the door to Bail's truck and told him that it was okay. Only then did Bails move.

When Bails got to the back door to the home he saw the door open. Sandy stood there welcoming him into their home. He came inside and told Dan that he needed to talk to them all.

Bails told Dan, Sandy, and Evie about the four spies that Major Gillis had already sent. By this time the four spies were set up in a home just half a mile from Dan's Compound. The only information that Bails did not have were pictures of the spies. He had their names so Dan sent out his own spies into the town looking for any new people in town with those names. As Gillis' spies made themselves known to the townspeople Dan's spies would quickly found them and pretended to make friends with them. A spy war had begun in that small Texas town.

That evening Dan's spies came back to him with the information that they had collected. They even knew where the government spies had rented their home. All of this information was written down by Sandy who had become Dan's Adjutant.

Dan called Davis into the kitchen. When Davis got there Dan talked with him for a while and told him about the four government spies sent by Major Gillis. This was a great time to give the trainees some field testing.

By this time Davis only had nine trainees left; one of which was his cousin Robert. Davis did not know that Robert was looking for a way to make some good money off of what he had learned about little Mary Ann. When the trainees were told what they would be doing the next day Robert found his chance to get rich.

That night those in the Compound relaxed as the Trainees prepared to go into town the next morning. Mary Ann played with her doll on the bedroom floor while her mom watched the TV from bed. Suddenly Mary Ann stopped playing and looked towards the bedroom door. Evie noticed the sudden movement and asked Mary Ann what was wrong.

"Something is wrong." she said quietly. "I can feel it."

"Is this one of your abilities?"

"I don't know … Mom." Mary Ann whispered. "Someone here is …"

"Is what Baby Doll."

"Someone here is planning to go against Uncle Dan."

"In what way?" Evie asked.

"I don't know." Mary Ann said. "But … someone is hiding a secret … a secret that will hurt us all."

Evie instantly went downstairs and talked with Dan. Then they got with Sandy and Davis. At the kitchen table the four discussed what Mary Ann had told her mother. When Mary Ann came into the kitchen Dan asked her a few questions.

"Do you know who it was that has this secret?" Dan asked her.

Mary Ann thought for a while and then said; "I don't know

Uncle Dan."

Dan told Mary Ann that everything would be okay and advised her to go on to bed. As she walked upstairs Evie fallowed. The two slept most of the night but Mary Ann continued to walk up from time to time during the night. What she felt nagged at her like an animal chewing on tough leather. By morning her fear had turned to anger. She did not like someone that was a danger to her family and friends. And now it was one of her friends; someone there that was the threat.

The next morning Mary Ann stood by the back door as the trainees walked out to the trucks that would take them into town. They were all dressed in dirty work clothes so they would look like one of the farmers or ranchers coming into town to get something. As they walked out of the back door of the home one by one Mary Ann closed her eyes.

Suddenly Mary Ann yelled: "You!" as she opened her eyes and looked up. "It's you."

Instantly Davis pulled his cousin Robert aside and ordered the others to continue. "You stay here today."

"I don't have …"

"You will fallow orders." Davis yelled. "Do you understand me?"

Robert looked down knowing that he would get another chance. "Yes Sir."

The others continued to load into the three trucks. Then Davis drove one truck into town and they were dropped off in different places. Many of the people in town knew Davis so he came back to the Compound. He had his cousin to deal with.

As soon as Davis drove into the back yard and pulled up close to the back door Robert walked out and met him. "Why did you have me stay here?" Robert asked loudly.

"Come inside." Davis said as he waved for two of the regular soldiers to also fallow them.

Davis and Robert sat at the table. Davis told the two soldiers to shoot Robert if he tried running away. They agreed with a quick "Yes Sir" and then spread out. Robert sat there with his mouth open wondering what was going on.

"What's wrong?" Robert asked Davis.

"We think that you might be planning something bad for all of us here in the Compound." Davis explained.

"Does this have anything to do with that girl yelling at me this morning?"

"A little bit ... yes." Davis said as Dan walked into the kitchen and sat down close to Davis.

"That girl can since when things are not right." Dan advised Robert. "And she called out when you walked by her this morning."

Robert pretended to not know what Davis was talking about. "I don't know what it could be though. I just want to do well here and change my life around. We talked about this." he told Davis.

Davis let out a heavy sigh and looked at Dan. "Could Mary Ann have been wrong?"

"I don't know." Dan replied. "She's never done this before."

"I think we need to talk to Mary Ann again." Davis suggested to Dan. Then he looked at Robert and added; "In the meantime you stay on the compound."

Dan asked Robert to leave. Then he called out for Evie and Mary Ann not knowing that they were sitting in the den a few feet away. Evie yelled back as she laughed. She and Mary Ann got up from the couch and walked into the kitchen. After they sat down at the table the questions started.

"Mary Ann ..." Dan started. "Are you sure you feel something bad about Robert?"

"Yes Uncle Dan." she replied.

"This feeling you got about him ..." Davis mentioned. "Is it one of your ... powers or abilities?"

"I don't know." she answered as she started to cry.

"Don't cry Mary Ann." Dan said softly. "It's okay."

"I don't have any more questions Sir." Davis told Dan.

Evie took Mary Ann upstairs to take a nap. As soon as they were upstairs Dan and Davis continued to talk. Neither of them had any reason to hold Robert. Holding him just because Mary

Ann said that something was wrong was not a good enough reason. Davis called for Robert and then took him into town to scout out the government spies with the others.

Davis dropped Robert off with a couple of other trainees and then came back to the Compound. Before long the three met up with one of the government spies. His name was Mat. They talked for awhile and then went their own ways. It did not take long after that for Robert to wonder off by himself.

Robert left the other two saying that he had to use the restroom. Instead of going to the restroom he left the business out through their back door. The other two trainees waited for Robert in front of the business until they finally checked on him. When they discovered that he was gone they reported back to Dan by cell phone.

Dan was furious. He gave Robert a chance and now Evie and Mary Ann might be in danger. He called the others and had them keep an eye out for Robert. Two hours after disappearing Robert was spotted walking around the town. The trainees that found him went to him and kept him with them until Davis came back into town and got them all.

During the two hours that Robert was missing he had made contact with the same man that he and the other two had met earlier. He and Mat talked for a while before Robert started telling Mat what he knew. But he made sure that he did not tell everything. He wanted payment first. Then he would give the location of Mary Ann and her mother. Mat gave Robert his phone number and told him to call him the next time he was in town. Mat would have to talk with First Lieutenant Buford who would have to authorize the payment. The price for the information was half a million dollars.

Robert had not left Mat five minutes when the other two trainees found him. When the trainees got back to the Compound Dan and Davis questioned Robert.

"When you went into the restroom why did you leave out the backdoor knowing that the other two were waiting for you in front of the business?" Davis asked.

"I didn't know they were still there and you did tell us to spread out." Robert defended himself. "I just did what you wanted."

"Okay then." Dan said. "Go back to what ever Davis has for you to do."

"Why are you picking on me so much?" Robert asked.

"It's not just you." Davis advised. "Another one of the trainees disappeared for a while also." Of course Davis was lying but he did not want Robert to think that he was being singled out.

Robert went back to the barracks and lay down on his bunk. As he lay there he noticed that the others were not talking to him. None of them ever cared that much for him but they still sometimes talked with him. Robert was one of those kind of people that you called a friend but he was not really a friend. Friends help each other but Robert only helped himself.

Later Robert got out of his bunk and took a shower. The barracks had a Men's and Women's shower and restroom. None of the trainees said anything to him as he passed them. When he walked back by them as he left the shower they still said nothing to him. He knew that something was wrong and it had to do with much more than just the remarks of a child. All of the trainees knew who and what Mary Ann was so could this be a power that she had. Could she maybe read minds or feel his thoughts?

"What do you think we should do?" Davis asked Dan.

Dan thought for a moment and then replied; "There's nothing we can do. I can't judge a man on the feelings of a child even if it is Mary Ann."

"I agree." Davis said. "Robert has been showing signs of trying to change."

"Yes he has." Dan agreed. After thinking for a moment he added; "Maybe we should give him a chance but watch him as well."

"I agree." Davis said.

Davis went back to the barracks and told the trainees that they might be going back into town to try to get pictures of the government spies. The trainees only met two of them but got no pictures. The goal this time was to get pictures of them.

That night Dan and Davis called in one of the trainees. They chose Karrie because of her devotion to the group and understanding of the importance of keeping secrets.

As the three sat at the kitchen table Dan started. "Now for one thing, Kerrie, it is important that this conversation stays between us three only."

"I understand Sir." Kerrie agreed.

"Tomorrow when you all go into town your job will be to watch Robert." Davis advised her. "Still try to take pictures of the government spies but your main job will be to watch Robert."

"May I ask why you want me to watch him?"

Dan and Davis cleared their throats. Then Davis said; We have reasons to believe that he may not be as honest as we all think he is."

"None of the others like him to much but that's just because he's ... freaky." Kerrie said.

"What do you mean by freaky?" Dan asked.

"He's always quiet and very secretive." Kerrie advised. "He's just ... he's the kind of person that gets on your nerves just be being around. He does not have to say anything ... just be around you."

"Sounds like you understand our concern then." Davis said.

"I'll do whatever you want me to do Sir." Kerrie agreed.

"Thank you Kerrie." Dan said. "I'll remember this ... but you remember to keep this a secret forever. The others do not need to know that you were spying on one of them. They might stop trusting you."

"I understand Sir."

"Good. See you tomorrow morning." Dan said.

As Kerrie walked away Davis went to the front door. He made it a habit of looking out front from time to time. Although the Compound had a guard that just watched the front of the home Davis still had the need to look for himself. As he looked out of the window beside the front door he saw Robert talking on his cell phone in front of the barracks. Thinking nothing of it he

110

walked away.

What Davis did not know was that Robert was setting up another meeting with Mat.

"I was able to clear four hundred thousand dollars but not half a million." Mat said. "We don't have that much money around."

Robert thought for a moment. "Okay then … that's fine. I will be in town again tomorrow morning." Robert advised Mat. "All of the trainees will be in town trying to get pictures of you four. We know all about you four but we have no pictures of any of you."

"Who told you about us?" Mat asked.

"Some Sergeant named … I think Bails."

"We have a Sergeant Bails that works for Major Gillis … our boss." Mat admitted.

"I think that's him." Robert said. "This … Sergeant Bails learns things and then calls or comes here to tell Dan; my boss.

Robert went on to tell Mat all about the Compound as well as God's Soldiers and God's Angels. By time he finished he realized that he might have said to much. Mat might not pay him if he thought that Mary Ann was living at the Compound. So he added a little note that Mary Ann and her mother did not live there. After that Mat had no more questions. He would meet Robert the next morning with the money. But if Robert lied and the government spies did not find Mary Ann they would find him.

Chapter 11

Sweet Revenge

The next morning the trainees prepared for their trip into town. When they were ready they mustered in the kitchen. When they were all there they loaded into the trucks. Finally Davis came out and got behind the wheel of his truck. Then with a wave of Dan's hand they were off.

The three trucks dropped off their trainees in different parts of town. They all had their cell phones with them so they could use the cameras in them. Robert was to meet Mat in front of the drug store where he would get a briefcase with his money. The meeting time was set for 10:00 that morning. In trade he would hand Mat a single piece of paper with the address and a drawn map to the location of Mary Ann and her mother.

Robert knew that he would not be able to explain the briefcase so once he got it he would have to hide it until he got back to the Compound and got his truck. Then he would come back and get the money and leave town. None of the trainees were suppose to leave the Compound without permission from Dan or Davis but Robert figured that he could do it. All he had to do was jump into his truck and drive away.

After Davis dropped off the trainees in his truck he returned to the Compound. He and Dan would go back into town later to watch the trainees. They were still training. When Davis walked into the back door of the home he found Dan, Sandy, and Evie sitting at the table with their morning coffee. Davis joined them with his own cup of coffee.

In town Kerrie kept out of sight. She noticed that Robert was looking around more than normal. Robert worked his way around town until he got to the drug store. After looking around he stepped behind the building. A few minutes later a car drove around the building and pulled up to Robert. When the driver's side window came down Robert could see that it was Mat.

"You sure that no one is watching us?" Mat asked.

"Don't think so." Robert was sure of himself.

"Here." Mat said as he shoved a briefcase out of the car window. "Four hundred thousand dollars."

Robert handed Mat a piece of paper. "There is the address and a map as you wanted. She is at the Compound but the four of you aren't going to go in there and take that girl. To many guns there."

"We won't be going in at all." Mat advised Robert. "Someone else will be doing that."

"Well I'm out'a here." Robert said as he opened the briefcase and made sure it was full of money.

Without saying another word Mat put the car in drive and drove around the building and out of sight. Robert started walking the other direction. As he rounded the building he almost ran into Kerrie. She had been standing just around the corner listening to the conversation between Robert and Mat. With the briefcase in his left hand Robert quickly pulled a knife from his waist and swung at Kerrie's throat.

Kerrie did not move as a line of blood formed across her throat. Then she fell to the ground. Robert wasted no time walking to the front of the building. Before rounding the front corner of the building he looked back at Kerrie. She still lay on the ground not moving. He turned back and was off to hide the briefcase.

Luckily the slice to Kerrie's throat was not as bad as Robert thought. Otherwise he might have cut her again. A minute after Robert left an old woman drove around the back of the drug store building to come up on the other side to the pick-up window. Seeing Kerrie laying on the ground she hit the breaks. Another minute later an ambulance drove up. By this time two of the other trainees were there to see what had happened.

"It's Kerrie." one of the trainees told the other.

"Call Dan." the other trainee advised.

Seconds later; "This is Dan." he said on his cell phone.

"Sir." the trainee said. "We are behind the drug store where an ambulance is picking up Kerrie. It looks like her throat is bleeding."

"Are you sure?" Dan asked.

"They have gauze over her throat but it is bloody."

"No. I mean are you sure it is Kerrie?" Dan asked.

"Yes Sir. There is no doubt."

"Okay then. Get the others and get back to the Compound."

"Yes Sir." the trainee acknowledged.

Dan called for Davis and then told him what had happened. Then he had Davis go pick up the remaining trainees. He also had Davis keep an eye out for Robert. Because of the sudden recall of the trainees Robert did not get a chance to hide the briefcase of money.

When Davis pulled up to get the remaining trainees he saw that Robert was one of them. The trainees loaded into Davis' truck and then they were on their way back to the Compound. Three of the trainees road in the back of the truck. Robert was one of them.

"Bought you a new briefcase?" one trainee asked Robert.

"Yeah!" Robert said with a smile. "This one has more pockets."

As the truck hit a pothole in the road the briefcase fell over. One of the trainees picked up the briefcase before Robert could grab it.

"It's heavy." the trainee commented about the briefcase.

"I bought a few other things and just put them in the briefcase." Robert suggested.

The rest of the ride back to the Compound was uneventful. Davis pulled his truck to the back of the home as he always did. As he stood beside his truck he noticed that Robert dropped his new briefcase. When the trainees walked into the back door of the home Davis noticed that the briefcase had left a dent in the dirt. The dirt was packed with vehicles driving over it. The briefcase had to have been heavier than a normal empty

114

briefcase. Davis instantly ran into the home and stopped Robert.

"What's in the briefcase Robert?" Davis asked.

Robert knew that something was up. "Just a few things I got when I bought the briefcase."

"Let me see what all you got." Davis suggested.

"I'm in a hurry."

With a wave of Davis' hand three of the trainees held up their pistols and pointed them at Robert. Davis had expected this and had the three trainees stand by in case he was right. Davis stepped over to Robert and took the briefcase from his hand.

"Let's go into Dan's office." Davis said as he lead the way with Robert behind him and the three trainees behind him. When they walked into Dan's office Robert saw that Dan was sitting behind his desk.

"Come in." Dan told everyone. Then he turned his attention to Robert. "Sit down Robert.

"How are you doing this morning Robert?" Dan asked.

"Something tells me that you don't really care how I am doing."

"Well … I may and I may not." Dan said as he turned the briefcase around on his desk. Then he opened the briefcase and gazed at the money. "This your money?"

"Yes Sir. Why?" Robert was actually telling the truth. It was his money; money that he had just earned.

"Trainee Kerrie was attacked behind the drug store today." Dan advised Robert. "You know anything about that?"

"No Sir." Robert looked shocked. "Is she okay?"

"Actually … she will be." Dan said looking right into Robert's eyes. "When she wakes up we'll know who did it."

"Do you all think I did it?" Robert continued to act innocent.

"Let's just say that you have been acting … weird the past few days." Dan said. We don't have a holding area or jail of any type but I need this man confined. Are there any suggestions?"

One of the trainees that did not like Robert at all suggested putting handcuffs on his ankle. A chain could be added to the other end of the handcuffs and the other end of the chain could be locked around a tree in the back yard.

"Now wait a minute." Robert yelled. "I'm not an animal. I'm not a dog to be chained to a tree."

"Davis." Dan said.

"Yes Sir."

"Chain Robert to the tree out back and make sure he has water." Dan ordered. "And trainees. Stay with Robert until he is chained to the tree and … if he tries to run … shoot him." Then he turned his attention to Robert. "Your briefcase will be locked in the gun vault."

With a wave of Dan's hand Davis took Robert out to the large oak tree in the back yard. Then Dan got two other trainees and walked out to his truck. They got into his truck and drove down to the hospital. He drove around to the rear of the hospital and to the Emergence Room entrance. Once inside he found that Kerrie was on a gurney and being wheeled into a recovery room. When the nurses left the recovery room Dan and the two trainees went in.

Kerrie was still knocked out from the operation. "Stay with her." Dan ordered the trainees. Then he walked out to the desk to talk to someone about Kerrie. For a while he talked to one of the nurses there but they did not know much. Then he saw a doctor and walked over to him.

"Excuse me Sir." Dan said. When the doctor turned Dan recognized him as the surgeon that patched him up. "Ha Doctor."

"Mister Briks." the doctor said. "How have you been doing?"

"Oh I'm fine but I have a young lady over there. She works for me."

"You mean Miss Warks?"

"Yes Sir." Dan said. "How is she?"

"Well … who ever tried to kill her did not do the job." the doctor suggested. "They cut her throat but almost missed the jugulars. The left jugular was cut just enough to cause her to loose a great deal of blood but we got fresh blood back in her quick enough. The right jugular was barely cut. It did not bleed much."

"So she'll be okay?"

"Oh yes ... after two or three weeks of rest." the doctor advised.

"Sir." one of the trainees called out to Dan. "She's awake."

Dan and the doctor walked into the recovery room as the trainees walk out and stood outside the room.

"Don't try to talk." the doctor ordered Kerrie. As the doctor looked at her throat she continued to point at Dan.

When the doctor was finished he stepped out of he room. Dan got close to her and told her not to speak. "Just nod your head. Do you know who did this?"

Kerrie could just barely move her head as she nodded to say yes.

"Was if Robert?"

Again she nodded to say yes. She tried to tell Dan what she had heard but the little sound that came out did not make since. Then she pulled Dan's head close to her mouth. Unable to talk she knew that she could still whisper. Whispering she told Dan about Robert's meeting with one of the spies sent by Major Gillis. Then she told Dan something that he really did not want to hear. The government now knew where Mary Ann was and the spy paid Robert for the information.

"You stay here and watch over her." Dan ordered the one of the trainees. He told the other one to go back with him.

Dan and the one trainee went back to the Compound. He called for Davis to meet him in his office. When Davis walked into the office Dan old him to sit down. Dan then told Davis all that Kerrie had whispered in his ear. He wanted Davis to get Mary Ann and Evie out of there and into a safe house. Until a safe house could be found Davis was to put the two into a motel room guarded by three guards at all times.

Dan went out to talk to Robert. "Kerrie just told me that you were the one that slit her throat. Just tell me why and I'll let you go. But ... tell me the truth."

"Okay then." Robert agreed. "She saw me taking the money from Mat. She heard our conversation. She was spying on me."

"Who is this Mat?"

"He works for the government." Robert replied. "They were looking for that brat kid and her mother."

"That brat kid is named Mary Ann." Dan said through his teeth. "And just how much did they pay you for this information?"

"Four hundred thousand." Dan turned and started to walk away. "You said you would let me go if I told you."

With a quick glance back Dan asked; "And you believed me?"

A few hours later Davis had Mary Ann and Evie in a local motel with two of God's Angels guarding them. Two trainees were placed in a van just outside the motel room. If anything happened they would jump out of the van with their M-16's.

Mary Ann was enjoying the motel room but Evie did not like being confined to the room. Within four days Davis found a home and paid the first month's rent. Driving Mary Ann and her mother from the motel to the safe house had them driving right through the small Texas town. He had them get low so that no one would see them.

Finally they got to the safe house. Davis took Mary Ann and Evie into the home. Three of God's Angels fallowed. God's Angels were dressed in civilian clothing and their rifles were in gun cases. By time Davis and the three Angels had his truck empty two other trucks from the Compound pulled up. They were loaded down with food and supplies. It only took thirty minutes to unload the two trucks. Unpacking the boxes took another five hours.

The three members of God's Angels would take turns staying awake and guarding Mary Ann and her mother. They would only wear civilian clothes and even take care of the yard. Sergeant Bensy even planned to plant flowers in the small flower bed in front of the home. As far as anyone knew they were just another family that moved into the town.

Sergeant Bensy and one of the other men pretended to be man and wife but she was in charge of the mission. As far as the neighbors were concerned the other man in the group was the brother of the other man. Mary Ann and her mother were not to go outside for any reason.

Back at the Compound Robert had been chained to the large oak tree just outside the back door of the home for almost a week. He was given food twice a day and enough water to keep him not wanting more. One of God's Soldiers watched over him at all times just to make sure that he did not escape.

Kerrie finally got out of the hospital and rested in the barracks. On the same day that Mary Ann and her mother went into the safe house Kerrie got out of bed against her doctor's orders. She walked through the home with her dagger in hand. Dan and Davis sat at the kitchen table and watched her as she walked by and them and on to the outside. Seeing the dagger in her hand they got up and fallowed her out to the tree where Robert was.

"Don't do this Kerrie." Davis ordered her but she continued to walk towards Robert.

Kerrie stood over Robert and looked at him.

"You can't let her do this." Robert yelled. "Stop her."

Kerrie quickly squatted and put her dagger against Robert's throat. "Now you will know what it feels like to have your throat cut." Then she quickly slid the blade of her dagger against his throat cutting his throat but neither jugular vein.

As Robert choked on the blood that slowly ran into his throat Kerrie stood and stepped away from Robert. As she passed Dan and Davis she said; "He'll live."

Dan and Davis quickly went to Robert and saw that only his throat was cut. It was nothing serious but Doc would have to tend to the wound. As Kerrie walked back to the barracks Davis got Doc. Kerrie went straight to her bunk and returned her dagger to it's sheath. Then she lay back down and took it easy.

Without moving Robert indoors Doc gave him a local shot to deaden the area and sewed his throat up. It took five stitches inside and seven outside. Then he placed a bandage over the stitches to keep it clean while he was kept outside.

119

"Looks good enough since we are going to kill him anyway." one of God's Angels said.

Dan and Davis said nothing to the man that made the comment as he continued patrolling the area. Robert could not speak. His larynx had not been cut but talking was just to painful.

Dan and Davis walked back into the kitchen and got more coffee. Then they sat down at the table to talk. They had to do something with Robert but what?"

"We could just take him out to the woods and shoot him." Davis suggested.

"Let the animals have at his body after that." Dan commented.

"The wild hogs would have a field day."

"You know ... that was the biggest problem that both sides had during the Civil War." Dan advised.

"What's that Sir?"

"Both sides had a problem with wild hogs eating the dead before they could be buried. Sometimes badly wounded men that could not defend themselves were eaten alive."

"Wow!" Davis chuckled. "I didn't know that."

"But what to do with Robert?" Dan remarked.

"You know ..." Davis said with a big smile. "You could just let Kerrie at him."

Dan thought for a moment. "I like the way you think. Take a few of the men and take Robert into the woods. Then tie him with his arms and legs opened wide. I don't want Kerrie hurt any more than she already is. Let me know when you're ready and I'll bring her out to you."

"Yes Sir." Davis was happy to see that his cousin would be killed for what he did to Kerrie. He never did have much respect for Robert. They might have been cousins but Robert had always been the black sheep of the family and he did not even care that he was thought of that way. Now it was time to end this nightmare.

Davis got four of the trainees outside by the large tree where

Robert was. As Davis unlocked the chain from the tree the others held onto Robert and walked him out into the woods. After realizing where they were going Robert realized that he was being taken into the woods to be beat almost to death or just killed. He had no idea what was in store for him.

Robert fought the four trainees but they held on. Finally they reached a spot where Davis found two trees to tie him to. As the trainees held Robert down on the ground Davis tied one rope to Robert's right wrist and the other end of the rope to one of the two trees. Then he did the same with Robert's left wrist. Pulling the rope tight Robert screamed out in pain. As the trainees held onto Robert's legs Davis tied ropes around his ankles and the other ends to the ropes to two other trees. Now Robert lay on his back on the ground with his arms and legs spread out.

Robert continued to yell so Davis tied a rag around his mouth. He did not want Robert's yelling to cause neighbors to call the police. The neighbors on both sides of the Compound did not like Dan and his, "army", as some called them. The police got so many calls from Dan's neighbors that they stopped coming out unless there was a really bad complaint.

"We're ready Sir." Davis said over his hand held radio.

"Okay." Dan replied. "We'll be right there."

About thirty minutes later Dan and Kerrie walked up to the group in the woods. Dan made sure that Kerrie saw Robert and then handed her a knife.

"Have fun." Dan said as Kerrie walked towards Robert with a smile on her face.

Calmly Kerrie cut off Robert's pants. He tried to scream but the gag in his mouth kept him from doing it. Robert was never circumcised as a child so Kerrie started by taking care of that. Then she continued to remove his private parts; a little piece at a time. After cutting off his shirt she removed his nipples. Then she worked her way up to his ears and removed them as well.

As Kerrie continued to cut parts of Robert's body the others there cringed at her sadistic savagery. Two of the trainees started to walk away but Dan stopped them.

"You'll be learning how to do this as part of your training; so watch." Dan told them.

"We'll be torturing people?" one asked.

"Let's say your enemy tortures one of you to death but it took a few days for him to die." Dan advised. "During those two or three days you had to listen to his screams. Then you capture one of the enemy. Wouldn't it be nice to know how to torture him but keep him alive while you're doing it? Now watch and learn. Kerrie is a master at this."

The two trainees stopped and fallowed the orders given to them. Kerrie was not only a master at torturing tactics but she was the one that trained the trainees in it. Thirty minutes after Kerrie started cutting on Robert she ended it with a quick slash to his throat. This time she cut the jugular veins.

Everyone there stared at Robert as he bled to death. Slicing his throat really did not matter as he had almost bled to death before that. All around Robert's body the grass and ground was blood red.

"What do we do now Sir?" one of the trainees asked Dan.

"Take the ropes off of him and let the animals have at him now."

"Yes Sir." the trainee said as he and the other three removed the ropes from Robert's body.

Then they all went back to the home and continued to do what they were doing that day. Davis and the trainees went back to training. Dan and Kerrie went into the kitchen and got themselves a big glass of ice tea. It was not quite mid April and while the mornings were still cool the days were getting warmer.

Dan smiled as he thought about his wife Sandy The baby was due in about a month. He had feared being a father but now he looked forward to it.

Chapter 12

Welcome Home

As Dan and Kerrie sat at the table drinking their ice tea one of the security brought Sergeant McNeil to them. Then Kerrie got up and washed the blood off of her arms and hands.

"Well good morning McNeil." Dan said as he stuck out his hand.

McNeil shook Dan's hand and then told him; I have a warrant for your arrest Dan."

"What for?"

"For being ugly." McNeil tried to look serious but a smile finally formed on his face.

Dan smiled. "You're a nut. You know that right?"

McNeil sat at the table and said; "Actually I have a few questions for Miss Marks here."

"Don't let me stop you." Dan replied.

All of McNeil's questions had to do with her being hurt behind the drugstore. Kerrie had not answers until he asked her why she was behind the drugstore in the first place. She knew that she had to think before answering.

"I thought I saw Davis back there but I ended up walking into a … I think a drug deal. One of the men jumped at me and cut my throat. He must have thought that I was dead and left me laying there. Then I woke up in that recovery room in the hospital."

"And where did the blood on your shirt come from?"

"We butchered a rabbit this morning. It was a class I was teaching the trainees. This is part of their survival training."

Kerrie cleared her throat and held her throat. McNeil knew that it was hurting her to talk so he cut it short.

McNeil excepted her answer and continued to ask a few more

questions. Then he said he was finished and thanked Kerrie for her cooperation. He and Dan talked for a while but McNeil had to leave as he continued his investigation.

"I'll find out who did this to you Kerrie." McNeil promised.

When McNeil left Dan knew that he had to do something with Robert's body. With that in mind he called for Davis again. A few minutes later Davis walked into the kitchen.

"Yes Sir." Davis reported.

"We need to get rid of Robert's body." Dan said. "Got any ideas?"

"We have all of those treetops back there that need to be burned." Davis suggested. "We could pile them on top of his body and burn him up. There's plenty of treetops to finish the job."

"Kill two birds with the same stone." Dan said with a smile.

"And it will give the trainees some exercise." Davis advised.

"Of course. A third bird." Dan replied.

Davis called all of the trainees together except Kerrie. Then he took them out to Robert's body. Once there he ordered them to put the tree branches on top of Robert's body. As the trainees continued to add the tree branches Davis set the pile on fire. Before long a large blaze could be seen from the house. It got so hot that the trainees had to stop adding branches until the fire burned down some. When the sun started to set Davis had two of the trainees remain to continue adding branches to the fire. Others would relieve them throughout the night.

When Davis got up the next morning he got a cup of coffee and walked out to the still burning fire. There was still plenty of wood left to burn so he had the trainees continue to burn it. The fire had burned down a great deal so that Davis could look into it. With only a few branches still burning he could see the red hot ground but no hint of any body being burned. He ordered the trainees to continue and then walked back to the house.

By time Davis walked back into the kitchen Dan and Sandy were sitting at the table. After refilling his cup he sat down with them.

"You checked on the safe house yet?" Dan asked.

"No Sir." Davis replied. "I just got up and checked the fire back there."

"Oh yes. How is it going?" Dan asked.

"The fire died down enough that I could see nothing left except some burning wood." Davis advised. "I had the trainees continue clearing the area of the branches. They should be finished this evening some time."

"Sounds great." Dan said. "I'll check on the safe house."

"Then I'll get the rest of the trainees out there to finish the burning."

"Sounds great." Dan replied. Then he got up and walked into the Computer and Radio Room. From there he called the safe house which was only about three miles from the Compound. The radio that they had at the safe house was not like the HAM hand held radios that they used on the Compound. They were only good for about one and a quarter miles. For long distances they used regular military radios which a soldier carried on his back.

Dan was kicking off his campaign for County Judge. He still did not have enough members of God's Soldiers to be going on any missions. This would have given him the money for his campaign. He would have to dip into his private funds for this. In the meantime he put the word out that he was still recruiting for God's Soldiers.

The trainees graduated early but would continue their training on the job. Finally they were free to do as they wished; to come and go as long as they were not on duty or training. As trainees they were not allowed to carry loaded pistols but now they did. All but one of the trainees had their CHL but Davis was trying to help the last one get his.

The problem was that Texas would not give the man his CHL because he wrote seven bad checks over thirty nine years earlier. He also paid them off thirty nine years earlier. Texas would not excuse this so Davis contacted the Arizona CHL Department. They sent the man an application. Within thirty days the man had his Arizona CHL.

Dan was busy with his campaign for County Judge and

excited about the baby being due any day. He worried about Mary Ann and Evie being safe and the government that may attack the Compound at any time.

Americans think that they are so safe. The Bill of Rights will protect them. But that is not true. If the government wants you bad enough then they will come in with a horde of soldiers and grab you without a warrant. That's what happened to Michael; Evie's husband and Mary Ann's father. All of the time American citizens pop up missing and are never heard from again.

Back at Fort Hood Major Gillis was planning his own personal attack in order to grab Mary Ann and her mother. He already had a company of soldiers standing by awaiting his orders. Those at the Compound would not stand a chance against one hundred twenty well armed soldiers. Everything was set. Major Gillis would attack Dan's Compound in mid May.

Bails found out about the attack that Gillis was planning and was getting ready to warn Dan when he was arrested. The spies that Gillis had sent into the small Texas town to find Mary Ann told him what Robert said about Sergeant Bails. With Bails being held at Fort Hood Dan had no idea of what was coming.

Including the new members of God's Angels Dan only had fifteen ready to fight. Kerrie was insisting that she was ready but Dan ordered her to stand down unless she was needed.

Finally the day came when Sandy went into labor. Dan drove her to the hospital taking two guards with them. This left only thirteen guarding the Compound.

Sandy was taken into an examination room where she was looked over by the doctor. The baby's head was already showing so she was rushed into the delivery room. Over the next five hours Dan almost went crazy not knowing that a woman's first birth was usually a long one. Finally the top of the baby's head could be seen.

"Now my first concern is the baby and then the mother." the doctor told Dan. "If you pass out we will walk on you if we have to. You are our last concern."

"Blood doesn't bother me." Dan advised.

"Then lets go get your baby." the doctor said with a big smile.

The doctor placed Dan at Sandy's head and advised him to help her sit up when he called for it. After helping Sandy sit up four times Dan heard someone get slapped and then the cry of a baby. His eyes had been fixed on Sandy's face but he now looked up to see his son being laid on Sandy's chest. Then the doctor asked Dan if he would like to cut the umbilical cord. The doctor handed Dan a pair of surgical scissors and pointed to where he was to cut.

After Dan cut the umbilical cord the baby was taken away to be cleaned and wrapped up. This was when they also circumcised him by using a tight rubber band. Then it was placed in a tiny bed in the Maternity Ward. Dan and Sandy would see their son again at feeding time.

Sandy was cleaned up and then wheeled to a private room. Dan needed some fresh air and walked around for a while thanking God for his son. Then he saw a few gurneys being rolled into the Emergency Room. Thinking nothing of it he walked by a couple of the gurneys and noticed that they both had two of God's Angels on them. They were left in the hallway because the ones hurt the most were being worked on.

"What happened?" Dan asked one of the men on the gurney.

"The government attacked the Compound." the man told Dan. "They tried to get Mary Ann and her mother but they were not there."

Dan ran back to Sandy and told her what happened. She understood that he had to go back to the Compound. As he left her she prayed for him and the others.

"Father … he really needs you right now. I'm okay. You took good care of me and our son but Dan needs you right now."

Dan quickly drove to the safe house to make sure that Mary Ann and Evie were safe. As he slid to a stop in front of the house one of the guards came outside. Dan ran up to the guard and ordered him inside. After slamming the door shut Dan told them all what happened.

"But no one called us from the Compound on the radio or by phone." Bensy said. "When did this happen?"

"I don't know yet." Dan advised. "Sandy just gave birth to our son and gurneys started coming into the hospital with our people on them. I'm headed out to the Compound now but I need you three to keep them safe."

"Will do Sir." Bensy said.

Dan ran out to his truck and jumped in. Then he was off to the Compound. When he arrived he found four ambulances still loading the wounded. All of the town's police cars were there as well. Dan drove around to the back of the home and slid to a stop sideways. He jumped out of the truck and ran to the back door to the home where he was met by McNeil.

"Slow down there cowboy." McNeil said. "I don't need you messing up evidence. Now take a breath and calm down."

Dan took a few deep breaths and calmed down. "I know who did this."

"Who?" McNeil asked.

"The government ... Major Gillis to be exact." Dan said as he was still trying to calm down. "By the way. Sandy had our little boy."

"Congratulations." McNeil said. "Now you have someone else to train."

"I already bought his first rifle." Dan said. "I need to check on my people and on any damage."

"Go ahead but watch out for orange cups covering evidence on the floor."

"No problem." Dan said as he stepped inside the home.

Everything looked normal in the kitchen but the den was another story. Orange cups must have covered over one hundred bullet casings. *One hell of a firefight went on in there.* dan thought to himself. As he walked towards the front door Davis walked in.

"Thank God you're okay." Dan said.

"Not really." Davis advised. "I got shot in the left hand."

"Get to the hospital and get that taken care of." Dan ordered him.

"I can't do that Sir." Davis argued. "You know that I would just be standing there or laying on some gurney while they took care of everyone else. I am more useful here right now."

"You're right but … don't wait to long."

"Yes Sir."

"What's the damage?" Dan asked Davis.

"We only had thirteen here not including me. Luckily we only lost six with three others badly hurt at the hospital." Then Davis looked at Dan and asked; "How is Sandy?'

"She had a little boy." Dan told Davis. "Then a bunch of gurneys started coming in with our people on them."

"How about Mary Ann and her mom?"

"I went there before coming here. They are fine and did not even know this had happened. They are all okay."

Dan walked around the inside of the home and then out front where two of the dead Angels lay. "She was very promising." he said as he pointed at one of the dead.

"Well she died fighting like a soldier." Davis said just above a whisper.

"Okay." Dan said trying to take it all in. "I need to get back to Sandy and I need to check on all of the wounded. I need you to take care of things here."

"In case you have not been told yet … they came in shooting." Davis said almost crying. "If Mary Ann had been here they probably would have killed her."

"Well there will be some retaliation for this." Dan insisted. "That Major Gillis is a dead man. His body just does not know it yet."

"I'll be okay now." Davis said. "You get back to the hospital. Sandy needs you right now."

I doubt if Gillis will come back here anytime soon so call the safe house. Have everyone brought back here. I think Evie and Mary Ann will be safe here now and you need the other three here."

"I'll call them on the radio Sir."

"Okay then. I'm out'a here." Dan said as he walked out to his truck. In seconds he was on his way back to the hospital.

Davis went into the radio room and called the safe house. He told them that Dan had ordered all of them to get back to the Compound. They would wait until it was dark and then move back. That was fine with Davis.

When Dan got back to the hospital he first checked on Sandy. She was sleeping so he went on to check on all of the wounded. Four of them were in hospital rooms with bad injuries but all would live. One other stood by with another Angel. He had only been shot in the arm and would be released that evening.

"How's your arm?" Dan asked the man that was standing.

"Oh I'll be okay Sir. The bullet went through and did not hit the bone." Then the man grabbed Dan's arm. "We all did our jobs but there were to many of them. There must have been an entire company of soldiers hitting the Compound."

"I know. You all did what you could but I need you all to heal up. We're going to hit them back."

"But aren't they out of Fort Hood?"

"That's why I need you all to heal up first." Dan advised. "Keep this a secret though."

"Yes Sir." the man acknowledged. "This is something that I think we all will be wanting to help you with."

"Well I need to get back to my wife now."

"How is she doing Sir?" the man asked.

"She gave birth about two hours ago to a boy."

"Alright." the man replied.

Dan left the wounded and went back to Sandy. This time he was stopped in the hallway while the babies were being taken to their mothers. It was hospital policy. Finally he was able to continue on to Sandy's room. She had the option to use a bottle or breast feed the baby. She chose to breast feed.

"What do you want to name him?" Dan asked Sandy.

"I was thinking Danny Moris Briks … if you don't mind." Sandy said.

"No problem here Babe." Dan agreed.

Dan stayed with Sandy until the babies were returned to the Maternity Ward and visiting hours were over. On his way back to the Compound he dropped by the safe house to make sure it was still locked up. To much equipment was still in there. Finding the safe house all locked up he got backing his truck and drove to the Compound.

After pulling around to the back of the home he found Mary Ann running out to him.

"Hi Uncle Dan." Mary Ann yelled as she jumped into his arms.

"With all that has happened you need to get back inside and stay inside." he told her. "People are trying to kill you and your mom."

"Suddenly Mary Ann got mad. "Who is trying to kill us?"

"Some bad men that work for the government but don't worry. We're going to get even with them."

"Good." Mary Ann replied as she ran back in the home.

The next morning Dan woke up excited about Sandy and the baby coming home. As he walked into the kitchen he found Davis already there drinking coffee and reading the newspaper.

"Good morning Boss." Davis said as Dan was pouring his cup of coffee.

"Good morning." Dan replied.

"So the baby comes home today." Davis remarked.

Dan smiled. "That's right. Little Danny Moris Briks comes home today."

"How long are you going to wait before giving him his Ruger 10/22 rifle?"

"Oh … about five minutes." Dan said still smiling.

As Dan and Davis drank their coffee others came through and congratulated Dan. The coffee pot was a very large one so almost everyone stopped by to get a cup of coffee. Dan did not care as long as they did their job. For those not actually on duty the barracks also had a large coffee pot. Dan enjoyed those on duty coming by the kitchen to get their morning coffee so he could see who was on duty.

After three cups of coffee Dan got up to go get Sandy and, Little Dan, as everyone was already calling him. He said his good-by's to everyone there and then walked out to his truck. He opened the door to his truck and then stood there. Everything would change when he came back. Nothing would be the same. A little boy was coming into the picture.

Then Dan thought about the dangers that he was bringing his son in to. So many had been killed while trying to find Mary Ann and her mother. If Sandy and Little Dan had been there would they have also been killed. Defending the Compound suddenly took on a whole new meaning. Dan knew that he not only had to stop Major Gillis but; for the sake of his wife and son he had to stop the government from continuing their assaults on the Compound.

"Davis." Dan yelled out towards the house.

Davis came running outside with his pistol drawn thinking that someone was attacking Dan. After looking around and seeing no dangers he calmly said; "Yes Sir."

"We are going to attack Fort Hood but mainly that building where Major Gillis has his operation." Dan told Davis. "Start making plans. I'll be back in a few hours."

"Yes Sir." Davis happily said. He had been waiting a long time to hit that building and destroy it. However; they only had a few of God's Angels left. All of them were needed to protect the Compound as well as Dan's wife and new son.

Dan drove to the hospital and parked. Again he arrived while the babies were being taken to the mothers so he had to wait. For a small town the hospital still had three mothers and new babies including Sandy and Little Dan. Finally after what felt like an hour of waiting Dan was allowed to continue to Sandy's room.

Dan walked into the room and found his wife feeding Little Dan. He pulled the chair close to the bed so he could be closer to Sandy and Little Dan. Before long a nurse came and got Little Dan. It was time to get him ready for his trip home. A few minutes later the doctor came in and looked Sandy over. Then he said that she could go home as soon as he finished the paperwork.

It took the doctor just over two hours to finish his paperwork. A nurse came into Sandy's room with a wheelchair and got her. Then they went to the Maternity Ward and got Little Dan. Minutes later the nurse was helping Sandy and the baby into Dan's truck.

As Dan climbed into the driver's side he looked over at Sandy holding their son. With a big smile on his face he started the motor and drove out of the parking area of the hospital. On the way home Dan told Sandy about his fears of the government coming back. He worried mostly for her and Little Dan.

"Well … we do have that safe house." Sandy suggested. "It has four bedrooms … plenty enough for me and Little Dan, Evie and Mary Ann, and the guards."

"You're right." Dan said as he pulled over. Then he called Davis.

"Yes Sir." Davis said on his cell phone.

Dan told him that he needed three of God's Angels at the safe house as soon as possible. He was taking Sandy and Little Dan there at that time. When Dan drove up to the safe house he quickly rushed Sandy and Little Dan up to the front door. After unlocking the door he rushed them into the home and searched the home for anyone that might have broken in. The home was clear.

Sandy and Little Dan went into one of the rooms and climbed into the bed. A few minutes later Davis and the three members of God's Angels showed up. Many of the neighbors watched as three people dressed in camouflaged clothing and carrying M-16's ran into the home. Davis, also dressed in his camouflaged clothing fallowed them.

The first thing that Davis and the three guards did was check out Little Dan. Davis had the guards change clothes to look more like the civilians. Then he walked out to a small crowd of neighbors that saw them running in with their M-16's. He told them that they were just coming back from a National Guard exercise. The neighbors bought the story.

133

Dan would stay there with his wife and baby while Davis would run everything at the Compound. When ever Dan left Sergeant Bensy would be in charge of the safe house. With eight people being in the safe house including Dan they would have to work to keep the neighbors from talking. Evie and Mary Ann and, Sandy and little Dan would have to stay inside.

Mary Ann would have the hardest time at staying in the house. She needed her time outside getting the sun. However; it had not been long since the incident at the bar-b-q restaurant and many might still remember what she looked like. They did not need anyone recognizing her.

Chapter 13

Fort Hood

When Dan woke up the next morning he called Davis to see how he was doing on the attack plans. Getting into Fort Hood was one thing. Destroying the Satellite Building would be no problem.

Davis had one of God's Angels check on what had happened to Sergeant Bails. He had not been heard from in a while. A few days after the Angel went to Fort Hood he returned with bad news about Sergeant Bails. He told Dan that Bails had been arrested on espionage charges. He had been found guilty and executed for his crimes. This angered Dan even more.

Dan returned to the Compound to help in the planning of the attack on Fort Hood. As he and Davis talked Evie reminded Dan that Michael went into Fort Hood and the building the first time it was destroyed through the back fence.

"That's right." Dan said. "But he was alone and I am sending at least ten people in."

"Then I suggest that you go in through the front gate." Evie added.

Dan and Davis looked at each other and then started laughing.

"I'm serious." Evie insisted. "Go in and sabotage something." She smiled and added; "Then send in a team as military specialist that Gillis needs to repair his equipment. Then set explosives all over the building and level the place and kill everyone in it."

"Evie ..." Dan said. "I love the way you think."

Evie left the room for Dan and Davis to change everything they had planned. First they would have to get someone in to sabotage something like maybe something in the Satellite Room.

Dan spent the next week training three of the Angels to act

a technicians. Their main job would be to set explosives in and around the Satellite Room. Three other Angels would act as electricians checking blown breakers and fuses and burned wires. They would really be setting explosives throughout the building.

Finally the day came for the attack. A military pickup drove into the main gate and back to the Satellite Building. In the pickup were two of God's Angels. Their job was to sabotage the satellite receiver and monitor.

The two men went into the building where they showed their military identification cards and then went back to the Satellite Room. As they walked into the Satellite Room Lieutenant John Rubin jumped out of his chair and asked who they were.

"We have orders to clean the equipment in here." one of the Angels said.

"I didn't get any word on that being done." Rubin argued. Then he called Major Gillis.

"You know how sensitive that equipment is." Gillis told Rubin. "Just let'em do their job."

"Go ahead guys." Rubin told the two men.

One of the men got behind the control panel and started pretending to clean. He was looking for a wire that he could pull loose; something that would need to be soldered back. The other man cleaned the front of the control panel and kept Rubin busy with questions.

"So all of this is for one satellite to watch someone"

"That's about it." Rubin bragged. He was proud of his equipment.

"How does it work?" the man asked Rubin.

Before Rubin could answer the other man crawled out from behind the control panel. "You finished?" he asked the other man.

"No problem. This guy keeps this place clean."

The two men left the Satellite Room and then the building. After driving away in their truck the man that was keeping Rubin busy with questions asked the other one; "What did you do?"

"Most of the switches and buttons on that control panel have wires just plugged into the switches and buttons. I just unplugged a few of the wires and switched them around. I set the timer to turn the thing on in an hour. When it does the whole room will fill with smoke.

Just as the man said; an hour later the control panel turned on and the room quickly filled with smoke. Rubin quickly emptied a fire extinguisher into the back of the control Panel and turned it off.

The base fire department was there in less than three minutes and cleared the smoke that by that time had filled the whole building. Rubin looked behind the control panel and found that a few of the wires had burned. He called Gillis and told him about the damage. Having no other choice Gillis called for repairs to be done the next day.

Dan had already set up a connection with all calls coming out of the building. He allowed all of the calls to go through except when he heard Gillis calling the repair department.

"Repairs." Dan answered the phone.

"This is Major Gillis. I need some repairs on a control panel in the Satellite Room ... Building 360."

"No problem Sir. We can be there early tomorrow morning." Dan said.

"See you then." Gillis told who he thought was the real Repair Shop. That night the entire Satellite Room shut down and was locked up.

The next morning Dan lead the way with his Humvee with two other military pickups behind him. One of the pickups would be the electricians truck and the other one would be the satellite specialist. They drove to the back of the base where the Satellite Building was.

Getting past the guard at the front door was no problem with them using their military identification cards that Dan had made for each man. Dan informed the guard that his people would be going in and out all day carrying equipment. Then he went to the Satellite Room and found it still locked. When he went back to the front door guard he met Lieutenant Rubin just coming in to work. He fallowed Rubin back to the Satellite Room.

"You don't look familiar." Rubin told Dan.

"Your usual crew is off doing something else so they sent us." Dan replied.

Dan's job was to keep anyone that might cause his teams problems busy. His team had to work uninterrupted. For the time being that meant keeping Rubin busy so he would not check into what was going on.

Suddenly Dan felt a hand on his shoulder. He whipped around to see Major Gillis.

"You scared the dickens out'a me." Dan told Gillis.

With a smile Gillis waved for Dan to fallow him and then started walking away. When they got to Gillis' office they went in. Dan closed the door behind him.

"Can I help you with something Sir?" Dan asked Gillis.

"Yes you can by explaining one things to me."

"What is that Sir?" Dan asked.

"I didn't know that the repair crew had two teams." Gillis advised.

Dan had to do some quick thinking. "The base needed a second crew when you all built this building. We've been busy ever since."

"We have had our share of problems out here." Gillis admitted. "Okay then. That makes since I guess."

"Is that all Sir? My team has a lot of work to do and you need it done as quickly as possible … don't you?"

"Yes I do." Gillis admitted. "I know where she is but I still need to find her."

"Find who?" Dan asked knowing that he meant little Mary Ann.

Gillis realized that he had already said to much and said; "Oh nobody. It's not that important."

"May I get back to my work Sir?"

"Of course. I'm sorry I held you this long." Gillis apologized.

Dan stood and left the office. He informed both teams that

they did not have much time left. Over the next three hours explosives were placed inside the walls and behind every piece of equipment that looked important. Dan not only wanted to destroy the building he wanted to destroy everyone working there. In most cases an explosive was a small one equaling the blast of one grenade or less. They were designed to be small and easy to hide but just big enough to destroy a piece of equipment.

Finally the two teams were finished and gathered out by the trucks. It was time to leave. The explosives were all set to go off with the flip of a switch that was in Dan's Humvee.

"Wait here." Dan told the others. "There's something I have to do before we leave."

Dan turned and went back inside. With him and his team going in and out of the building the past few hours the guard just waved him on. He went straight to Major Gillis' office. As he stood in front of the door he thought about what he was doing and then knocked on the door.

"Come in." the Major said.

"We're finished." Dan told Major Gillis as he walked in. He closed the door but locked it without Gillis knowing. Then he bent over and pulled a pistol from a boot holster in his right boot. When he stood straight he held the pistol pointed at Gillis.

"This is for my wife, Mary Ann, and Bails."

Then Dan fired three shots into the chest of the Major. A silencer on the pistol kept anyone from hearing the shots. Dan turned and walked to the door and unlocked it. After opening the door he locked it again. Once in the hallway he closed the door and walked out to the others.

"Let's go." Dan told the others.

They all got in their vehicles and drove towards the main gate. The front gate sentry waved them through and they continued to the motel that they had called home for the past few days. After loading their things in the trucks they headed for the Compound.

Before leaving the motel Dan did one more thing that completed their mission. He raised the cover over a switch. After looking at his driver he flipped the switch but nothing happened.

Pull over." Dan ordered the driver. He got out of his Humvee and told the others to go on to the Compound. They were probably to far away for the switch to work. Then he told his driver to get in one of the other trucks. They did not like leaving Dan alone but he did not want them close by when the explosives went off.

The two trucks left for the Compound and Dan got behind the wheel of the Humvee. Making sure that it was clear he made a "U" turn and went back to about one hundred yards from the main gate. On the side of the road he held the switch box. Then he listened and flipped the switch. There was no sound of an explosion. He would have to go back into Fort Hood.

As he was waved through the gate he wondered why the explosives did not go off. He checked everything and the switch had a range of about half a mile. *What could be wrong?* he wondered. When he pulled over just two hundred yards from the Satellite Building he flipped the switch again and again nothing happened. Dan was never the one to panic but panicking was starting to look good at that time. Then an idea hit him. *The switch worked off of a single AAA battery. Was a battery in the switch box?*

Dan opened the switch box and looked inside. He thought it did not weigh enough. There was no battery in it. He search the truck for a AAA battery. Finally he found one but, was it still charged enough to do the job? He placed the battery in the switch box and closed it. He knew that if it worked he would have to get out of there quickly. *Should he go outside the gate and try it?* If the battery was not strong enough he would have to come back in to try it again. But if it worked then the gate sentry would close the gate upon hearing the explosion. He would be trapped.

Dan decided to drive to another building and try to get a good battery. He pulled over beside a building that looked like an office building and grabbed his multi-meter which he used to check electrical currents and other things. He went from office to office and finally found an office belonging to a Lieutenant that was over supplies.

"I think I have a package here in my desk." the Lieutenant told Dan.

"Oh I hope you do." Dan replied.

"Here they are." the Lieutenant said as he pulled out a small package of AAA batteries. "I need them for my clock on the wall."

Dan looked at the clock hanging on the wall and asked; "What do I owe you?"

"Oh nothing. Take it and good luck."

"Thanks a lot." Dan said as he shook the Lieutenant's hand. Then he went back out to his Humvee and put the battery in the switch box.

Suddenly there was a series of explosions at the back of the base. Dan realized that he did not flip the switch off before placing the battery in the switch box. Security at the base had been increased after the government took it back from the terrorist. Surely the gates were being closed by now and the two newly installed 50 caliber Brownings at the main gate were already manned.

Not wanting to be caught with the switch he took out the battery and then wiped his fingerprints off of it and the switch. Then he drove towards the front gate tossing the battery and switch out the window at two different spot.

As Dan pulled up to the gate he was surprised to find it still open and the 50 caliber Brownings were not manned. Although the sentry surely heard the explosion he did not know what it was. He probably just thought it was training of some kind. As the sentry waved Dan through the gate another sentry answered a phone call. As Dan drove down the road he looked back to see the gate closing and soldiers were manning the 50's.

A few hours later Dan drove onto the Compound and around to the back of the home. Everyone came out to meet him. It was already on the news that the terrorist had attacked Fort Hood again but no one knew just why they attacked only one building. The building had been totally destroyed and everyone in it was killed. A switch had been found which could have been used to set off the explosives but for the moment no one knew for sure.

Dan sat on the couch looking at the TV. *What makes a man want to kill another?* He thought to himself. *What drives a man like Gillis to go so far to capture a ten year old child? There had been so much destruction; so much death; and for what?* Dan continued to ponder these and many more questions. He tried to find a reasoning to it all. The government made Michael what he was and then locked him up because of their mistake. And then they went after his child; his little girl only because she was his child.

War changes a man into an animal but this was not even a war. It had been a skirmish between two different ideas; between two men and what they believed. But was it over now? Only God knew.

With Major Gillis dead and the Satellite Building totally destroyed Dan would now turn his attention to his campaign for County Judge. But he could not let his guard down in case there was still someone out there that wanted him or Mary Ann.

Dan got up from the couch and walked into his office. After turning on the TV in there he turned it to Fox News. They were not talking about Fort Hood but maybe it was just the local channels that were doing it for now. As the news got out even Fox News would surely start talking about it as well.

After doing a little research on his computer Dan got up and walked back into the den. He informed Davis that he was headed back to the home and to his wife and son.

Just as Dan started to drive off McNeil drove around the home and pulled up beside him.

"Howdy big guy." Dan said through the windows. Then he got out of his truck and walked to the front of the truck where he met McNeil.

"I have a few questions for you." McNeil said to Dan.

"Watch'a need?"

"Where is Evie and Mary Ann?"

"I have them at a safe house." Dan said with a smile.

"Where?"

"In this county." Dan was at the point that he did not trust anyone.

"Where in this county?" McNeil insisted.

"Every time I trust someone then people around me die." Dan said with his eyebrows lowered.

"It's me ... McNeil ... your friend."

Dan thought for a moment and then told McNeil the address of the safe house. He advised McNeil that Sandy and their newborn son were also there.

"Wouldn't they all be safer here?" McNeil asked.

"We used to think that until the military came through here with over a hundred men and almost wiped out my security." Dan said with anger in his voice. "Luckily Evie and Mary Ann were at the safe house at that time. Sandy and I were at the hospital giving birth to Little Dan."

"I'll make sure to have my officers patrol the area more often."

"Just don't tell them the address of the safe house or that there even is one." Dan insisted.

"No problem." McNeil said. "I'll tell them that there is an FBI operation going on in that area."

"Sounds good." Dan agreed.

The two men shook hands and got in their vehicles. Dan fallowed McNeil out of the Compound but at the road they went different ways. Dan went on to the safe house. When he pulled up to the curve in front of the safe house he was met by Sergeant Bensy.

"Good to see you again Sir." Bensy said.

"Good to see you too. I take it that everything is running smoothly?" Dan asked as they walked up to the house.

Bensy went back to planting cabbage in the front flowerbed. Dan walked into the house and straight back to the bedroom where Sandy and Little Dan were supposed to be. Finding the room empty he called out for Sandy. She and Little Dan were in the kitchen with Evie and Mary Ann. Dan got himself a cup of coffee and sat down at the table with the others.

"If I'm going to run for County Judge then I need to start campaigning. Not that many people in this county know me." Dan said.

"But the voters are tired of the County Judge we have now." Evie advised.

"Yeah I'd say so." Sandy added. "He's your typical Liberal Communist. He fills his pockets with our money while doing nothing but letting illegal aliens get away with murder."

"Literally." Dan said. "Remember that case about a year ago where an illegal alien out of Mexico murdered that family of four and this judge let him go free on a technicality. Then the Mexican bastard murdered another family and the judge let him go again."

"The voters are looking for someone that they can trust to keep them safe." Sandy commented. "This judge only keeps the criminals safe from prison."

Criminals and even good illegal aliens usually vote liberal so that is the reason these ... trash ... liberal communist set them free." Evie said.

"Well I've got to get busy." Dan admitted. "First I need to register and get on the ballets. Then I need to spend money ... a lot of it on campaign signs."

"A town hall meeting wouldn't hurt either." Evie said.

Dan's computer was back at the Compound so he kissed Sandy and Little Dan and left. He had a lot of work to do if he was going to run for County Judge.

What Dan did not expect was that the government was not through with their search for Mary Ann. Those with more power than the governor of Texas wanted her and her mother and nothing was going to stop them.

Chapter 14

The Overlords

There was a branch of the government that took it upon themselves to keep government experiments under control. These people were made up of a few Congressmen and Senators that got together and appointed themselves Overseers of experiments that they felt went wrong; such as with Michael. No one controlled them or governed how they operated. With Major Gillis dead and the Satellite Building totally destroyed these Overseers appointed another Colonel to take over the search of Michael's wife and child.

Colonel John Nathan was sent to Fort Hood to rebuild the Satellite Building and find little Mary Ann and her mother. Colonel Nathan looked at the leveled building and decided to rebuild it in a different location; maybe not even at Fort Hood. As he looked around he saw just how vulnerable the building was. Michael simply came in through the back fence and almost totaled the building. Then another group came in through the front gate and leveled the building. This place was not secure enough. He knew that he had to find another place to rebuild the Satellite Building.

Back at the Compound Dan was busy campaigning for County Judge. One thing bothered him about becoming a judge. If the government came back to look for Mary Ann would he be to busy as a judge to do anything about it? He talked to Sandy about this but she continued to support him as becoming the new County Judge.

One day McNeil came by the Compound so he and Dan could coordinate their campaigns and work together. Dan helped McNeil by paying for some of his campaign signs. They even set up a town hall meeting where they both would answer questions from the public. Time was not in their favor as the elections would take place in just over five months.

Colonel Nathan decided to rebuild the Satellite Building back at Fort Hood. However; this time the security would be much better than it had been in the past. He learned that the repair teams that came in to clean and repair the Satellite Room were not from the Fort Hood repair crew so they had to have been outside group. After doing a little research he learned about the invasion of Dan's Compound to find Mary Ann. Dan had to have been the one that came in and destroyed the Satellite Building.

This battle had become a personal fight between Colonel Nathan and Dan. Nathan did not want to attack Dan's Compound again but he had to take Dan down before he could find Mary Ann. When Nathan found out that Dan was running for County Judge he went to the town hall meeting in order to try to make Dan look bad.

Finally the day came for the town hall meeting. Evie and Mary Ann stayed at the safe house with the three members of God's Angels. Sandy and Little Dan went to the meeting with Dan. As they walked into the building many of those that knew Dan cheered for him. Most of the people there knew nothing about him though. Dan walked around shaking hands and telling everyone that he was happy to see them there.

The town hall meeting started with the local high school cheerleaders performing a few stunts. Then finally it was time and Dan was announced to speak. As he walked up on the stage many cheered for him. But what Dan did not know was that Colonel Nathan and four of his people were scattered throughout the crowd getting ready to destroy him.

Colonel Nathan and his people wore civilian clothes so they would look like the local people there. Even before Dan walked upon the stage to speak Nathan and his people were spreading vicious lies about him. They told others anything that they could think of to make Dan look bad.

Dan gave his speech which lasted only thirty minutes. Then he opened the floor for questions.

"Some say that when the military came into town a while back that they were looking for you. Is this true?"

"No Ma'am." Dan said with a smile. "They were looking for someone else. That used to live at my home."

"I heard that that Neanderthal girl was around here someplace and you were hiding her." one of Colonel Nathan's people asked.

"I heard that she is out there at your compound." Nathan himself added.

Dan held up his hands and calmed the crowd down. "I don't know much about this Neanderthal child but she is not at my place."

"Maybe you should allow some of us to come out to your place and see for ourselves." another one of Colonel Nathans's people said."

"I don't have to prove anything but ... I will allow three of you to come out to my place tomorrow and look for yourselves." Dan advised.

"Of course tomorrow." Nathan said. "After you move her out of there tonight."

Dan thought for a moment and said; "Three of you can go home with me tonight and look for her. Maybe that will ease your liberal communist mind."

"I'm not a Liberal." Nathan insisted.

"Okay then ... your Communist mind."

"Calling us voters names will never get you elected." one of Nathan's people said.

Dan turned his attention to the others there. "Does anyone have any questions about my being a judge?"

For the next hour Dan answered questions from the others there. As he answered his questions he noticed that Nathan and three others walked out of the town meeting together.

When the meeting was over he had won the votes of many of those that lived in the county. However; many others were still wondering if he was still going to allow anyone to go to his home and look for the Neanderthal Girl.

147

Before leaving Dan chose three reporters of local newspapers to go back to his home with him. As he worked his way out to his truck he shook every hand he could. By time he got to his truck the three reporters had pulled their vehicles up close to his truck. Finally Dan drove away with the three reporters close behind him. What Dan did not know was that one of the reporters was not a reporter. She worked for Colonel Nathan.

As Dan pulled around to the back of the home the reporters fallowed. Then they fallowed him in the back door and into the kitchen.

"My name is Janet. Do you really need all of this security?" the woman working for Nathan asked.

"Everyone with some money has security now days. Dan defended himself. "You know that."

Dan lead the three through the home and then back to the kitchen. Of course no little girl was found. Mary Ann was at the safe house. The three reporters were satisfied that Dan was not hiding the Neanderthal girl. However Janet found a few toys tucked away in the corner of the den.

"There must be a child someplace." Janet said as she pointed at the toys. "Who are these toys for?"

"My wife just had a baby and those toys are for when he gets older." Dan replied.

Why would you buy a doll for a boy?" Janet asked.

"Some of these toys are pass-me-downs from my sister before my son was born." Dan answered. "We did not know if we were going to have a boy or girl." Dan did not have a sister but his story was convincing.

The two reporters and Janet got back in their vehicles and left. The two reporters headed towards town but Dan noticed that Janet headed the other direction. There was something different about her but he could not put his finger on it. He had convinced the reporters that there was no child there except his son when Sandy got back with him. He told them that she was visiting a friend in Dallas.

Janet went straight back to Colonel Nathan. He had set his

people up in two motel rooms while they were there. When Janet arrived at the motel she walked right into Nathan's room which he shared with one of his people. Janet told Nathan what all was said and about everything she saw. Although she believed Dan's story about the doll Nathan did not.

"She's close by then." Nathan said. "She may not be at the Compound but she is close by ... someplace."

Colonel Nathan decided to hang around for a while and have his people talk to the local people in town. They could not only learn more about what was going on around there but they could spread more lies about Dan. He had one of his men sit in a truck down the road from the Compound and watch the Compound itself.

The next morning Dan got a phone call from a man that said he was part of Colonel Nathan's team in town. He was Sergeant Peter Flemings. Peter was about to get out of the military. He did not like what the military was doing with Mary Ann and her father. With this phone call to Dan he told Dan what was going on and opened the door to join God's Angels himself. But until he was out of the army he could only serve Dan as an informant. The more he helped Dan the closer he came to being able to join God's Angels.

Dan now knew that he had yet another enemy from the government. There was only one way to stop this. He had to go after the men at the top but, who were they? All Dan knew was that they were a few Congressmen and Senators and maybe a few men and women with plenty of money. These people took it on for themselves to take control of government experiments that went wrong. It was a nasty job that the government did not want so they allowed these self appointed Overlords to do it.

Dan knew about this thanks to his new friend Peter. But Peter did not know who they were or how many Overlords there were.

Dan had a meeting with Davis and a couple of his Angels. These two Angels were good at investigating things through the computer. First they made a list of possible people that might be the Overlords. Most Americans liked to brag about what they were doing so they searched Facebook and Twitter to start.

While the two Angels did their mojo on the computers Dan got back to his campaigning for County Judge. One month after the first town meeting Dan had another one. In this town hall meeting he would face off with the present County Judge as they both answered questions from the crowd.

On the morning of the second town hall meeting Dan got up early. After getting his coffee he sat on the couch to watch the local news. He did not care much for their news as it was always liberal biased. He mainly watched the local news for the weather reports. It was the only part of the local news where the truth was told.

The first thing that the news reporter did was talk about the battle for County Judge. The liberal biased reporter told a few stories about Dan which were complete lies. This is the one thing that Liberal Communist do well. Then the reporter went onto tell how that the present Judge sent many criminals to prison including terrorist and gang members which was another lie. The truth was that he let about ninety percent of them go free after committing numerous felonies. Dan would bring that up at the town hall meeting.

Being agitated at the lies being told by the local Liberal Communist Dan changed the TV to Fox News. *Finally the truth.* he thought to himself. But Fox News did not care much about small town politics and only mentioned the names of Dan and the present Judge.

Dan got up and went into the Radio Room where he had set up two computers for the Angels that were working on finding out just who the Overlords might be. The two women of God's Angels were already busy. Dan was amazed at how much they were finding. First they went through all of the Liberal Congressmen and Senators checking each one. Dan noticed on their list was the name of one Republican Senator.

"Who is this ... Republican?" Dan asked.

"He votes more like a Liberal than a Republican." one of the women said.

The women went on to tell Dan more about the Senator. The more he heard about this so called Republican Senator the more he hated him. Disgusted with what he was hearing Dan walked out into the back yard for a fresh breath of air.

God's Angels now had fifteen member and Davis was training another sixteen. He still had the money to pay his Angels but the campaign for Judge was quickly eating away at that money. He had lost most of his security jobs when the government came through the Compound and took out most of God's Angels. He simply did not have enough people to cover all of the security contracts.

Dan realized that he did not need God's Angels for any of the security contracts. He only needed qualified security that had their own Concealed Handgun Licenses. He put an add in a few of the local newspapers and within a week had more applicants than he could handle. These people would receive training there but they would just be highly trained security. None of them would know about Mary Ann and her mother. They would not be working at the Compound anyway.

With the added security at the Compound Dan had his wife and son, Evie and Mary Ann move back to the Compound. They would now be safer there than at the safe house.

With Evie taking care of Little Dan, that evening Dan and Sandy drove to the town hall meeting. Before Dan could pull into his reserved parking space a crowd gathered around him. Local police had to make people move so that Dan could park. At first Dan thought that these people were his supporters but most of them were not. As soon as Dan opened the door of his truck he was attacked by three young men.

The police pulled the three men off of Dan and arrested them for assault. Why is it that the young Liberal Communist think that laws never apply to them? Finally the police got Dan and Sandy into the building where they quickly got upon the stage. It was a fearful thirty minutes on the stage but finally the town hall meeting started.

151

The first one to speak was the incumbent Judge; Judge James Moore. He continued the same lies that the local liberal biased TV reporter said earlier. He bragged about how he had put away hundreds of criminals including a few terrorist and gang members and had almost wiped out the gangs in the area. When he finished he sat down so Dan could speak.

As Dan stood he was booed by almost every young punk in the building. It took a while but the police finally got them to be quiet. Those that would not be quiet were removed from the building. Finally Dan was allowed to speak.

"These young people that were making all of that noise were not really protesting me. They were trying to keep me from speaking. That is how the Communist work. That is why I call all Liberals ... Liberal Communist. Look at what the Communist want in order to take over our country. Now look at what the Liberals want. It's the same list starting with taking your guns."

The crowd cheered drowning out the young that were there. Most of the men and many of the women there were hunters. Cattle raisers needed rifles to defend their calves from wolves, cougars, and black panthers. Bobcats, coyotes, and fox were wiping out the chickens and rabbits in the area. Guns were a part of life to the people in the area and Judge Moore was trying to get them outlawed. He wanted the small county to be the first Sanctuary County in Texas.

"And Judge Moore talked about how he has imprisoned many terrorist and gang members. The truth is that he has freed over ninety percent of them including a mass murderer named John Biggs. Biggs wiped out three families ... sixteen people including seven children. He let Biggs go free only because the arresting police officer hit him. I ask you this. What would you have done if you were arresting a mass murderer like this?"

Again the crowd cheered and stood in approval. Dan felt good but he was not finished. He went on to tell those there that Judge Moore was bad for the community. He would only bring on more of what he had already brought.

"If for any other reason ... vote for me if you want to keep your guns. I want to allow those with CHL's to open carry. Let the criminals know that this county is not going to take their criminal activities. And if they commit crimes in this county then I will lock them away ... not throw them parties and let them go to kill more of you. I do not want a sanctuary county where only the criminals are safe ... safe from prison or any jail time."

When Dan finished speaking he got a standing ovation. Sandy stood beside him and with his arms around her Dan knew that he was going to win the election.

Over the past few weeks Mary Ann had been quiet. Something inside of her was bothering her. She knew about the people that were trying to get her and her mom. She just did not know of them as the Overlords. Dan had not yet mentioned the word. Mary Ann sometimes knew things that no one else knew; things that she was not told. Somehow; she just knew.

After returning to the Compound Dan went into the radio room to see the list of possible Overlords. The two women were off duty and sound asleep in the barracks. When Dan walked into the radio room he found Mary Ann looking at the list.

"Shouldn't you be in bed?" Dan asked Mary Ann.

Without looking up Mary Ann said; "I know which ones of these are your Overlords."

"How would you know?" Dan asked.

Mary Ann looked up at her Uncle Dan and said; "I don't know how I know. I just know."

"Well ... before I order the killing of these people I will need more than ... just your word. I know but ... at least mark their names before I go back to bed."

Dan took Mary Ann's advice and marked the names that she pointed out. As she left for bed he looked at the names that now had a check by them. Mary Ann did not mention if these were all of the Overlords or not. There might be more but at least he had names to start working with. Before going to bed himself he wrote a not to the two women working on the Overlord list telling them about the names that he had checked.

Within the next week the two women found four on the

153

Overlord list that had bragged about their actions on Facebook and Twitter. Using some bought and some stolen programs the women were able to intercept cell phone calls and e-mails proving that three more on the list were part of the Overlords. Another three looked very guilty but Dan was still not sure about them. Just to make sure that all of the Overlords were killed even these three would have to die as well.

Dan knew that if he did attack the Overlords all of them would have to be hit at one time. In this way they would not have time to run or hide after the first few were killed. He had the people to do it but half of them were still in training.

One evening Dan was working hard on locating the Overlords when McNeil dropped by to see him. They discussed their campaigns and then Dan told McNeil about Sergeant Flemings and the Overlords.

"You think you can keep this new war of yours out of my county … this time?" McNeil asked.

"This time I plan to take the war to them." Dan advised his friend.

"These … Overlords?" McNeil asked. "You're starting a war with people so powerful that they call themselves Overlords?"

"Yeah!"

McNeil cocked his head and raised his eyebrows as Dan walked by. "Okay. At least you're honest about it."

McNeil fallowed Dan out into the back yard where the God's Angels trainees and the new security force were training. The two groups were kept separate so that the security officers did not hear about Mary Ann. They would be used in security contracts such as body guards and other things. This would bring in more money for Dan campaigning.

McNeil left for his office. He had his own campaigning to do. The present sheriff had done a worse job than Judge Moore. Under his watch there had been three different escapes from the county jail. All thereof these escapes were known terrorist. Only the local Liberal Communist liked him.

As Davis walked up to Dan he said that the trainees were

doing well. Dan told Davis that they needed to get together soon concerning the Overlords. Then Dan and McNeil went back into the home where they both got a glass office tea and sat on the couch to talk. For the next hour they talked over their strategies to get Dan elected. The elections were still two months away but there was still much work to do.

Chapter 15

The Last Overlord

Over the next two months Dan learned a great deal about the Overlords. The two women found thirteen of them along with their addresses and daily habits. There was one thing that seamed to be common with all of the Overlords. They all felt and acted as if they were untouchable. Although they all had armed bodyguards this attitude of theirs made them easy targets.

The elections came and went. McNeil was elected as Sheriff and instantly started making changes. The previous liberal sheriff had left him a mess. Dan on the other hand did not get elected. Some say that the election was rigged but with what he had to do to stop the Overlords he did not care much about loosing the election. He was already busy.

Judge Moore starting working with the Liberal Communist of the county to outlaw guns. They went straight to fighting Dan and his armed security at the Compound.

A month earlier Dan had changed the training of God's Angels trainees to training them to attack the Overlords. By this time he had even more trainees which went straight to training to attack the Overlords. Some of the trainees were let go for different reasons. Finally Dan had enough members of God's Angels to send two of them after each Overlord. He changed their name to God's Soldiers.

As God's Angels left the Compound for their Overlord targets Dan kept Davis and Sergeant Bensy at the Compound. Peter Flemings finished his time in the army and came to the Compound. He had not only proven himself but Dan needed him there and allowed him to join God's Angels. He and seven others started their training. Peter was the only one of the trainees that knew about Mary Ann but he swore not to tell any of the other trainees.

God's Soldiers all went to their targets; the Overlord that they had been trained to kill. It was a Monday morning and all of the Overlord targets would be hit between nine that morning and noon. Each two person team would make their hit, quickly, leave the area, and then call Dan to let him know the job was done.

Dan was showing no mercy. He was tired of being hounded by these self appointed pompous asses. Completely destroying these people was the only answer left. He had tried hitting the men that worked for them and that did not stop them. There was nothing else to do.

In most of the cases the Overlord was simply shot along with any of their body guards that tried defending them. In one case an Overlord got into his car which a driver drove up in front of his home. As the car pulled away from the home one of God's Soldiers flipped a switch. The car blew up killing the Overlord and his driver.

Another Overlord walked out on his front steps awaiting her car to drive around and get her when her head seemed to blow up. A bullet from a fifty caliber rifle fired almost a quarter of a mile away ended her life.

Another Overlord walking through a crowd in New York city and stepped out of the crowd with a cut on his hand. Seconds later a poison caused him to have a heart attack. He was dead before he hit the ground.

By noon Dan had received phone calls from all of the members of God's Soldiers that he had sent out. All of the targets had been hit and eliminated and all of the teams had escaped.

Dan set back in his high back chair and sighed heavily. *Was this the end? Did we get all of the Overlords?* Dan questioned everything about this mission. Then he heard a voice beside him.

"There is still two of them left." Mary Ann said.

"How do you know?" he asked Mary Ann.

"I ... just know." Mary Ann said. "How many of the names that you put checks by were Overlords?"

"All of them and a few you didn't have me check." Dan replied.

"You still have two more Uncle Dan. " Mary Ann advised. "If you don't get them they will rebuild the Overlords and come looking for us again."

Mary Ann kissed her Uncle Dan on the cheek and then left him alone to think. For a long time Dan sat there thinking about what Mary Ann had said. It would take time to find the other two Overlords and by that time there would be more of them. Surely they would become much harder to find now. Knowing that he had to do something he sent two of the teams to Fort Hood. Their job was to hit two other target; Colonel Nathan and Captain Piles.

By the next day the four members of God's Soldiers were in the Fort Hood area. Using their fake military identification cards they went into the Fort Hood business offices. After a few minutes they found the home addresses of Colonel Nathan and Captain Piles. That evening as each man drove into the driveways of their homes members of God's Soldiers drove up behind them. All four of God's Soldiers emptied thirty round magazines with their M-16s riddling the men and their cars with holes. Before anyone could run outside to see what was going on the four members of God's Soldiers left. The only thing that two of the neighbors saw were pickup trucks with covered licenses plates.

About a mile down the road the two teams stopped and removed the duct tape covering the licenses plates. Then they separated and put as much distance between them and the men they just attacked as they could. That night all four of them drove into the Compound.

The four walked into the home and found Dan sitting on the couch watching the local news. There were already reports about the assassinations of Colonel Nathan and Captain Piles. A few reports mentioned other killings of some of the Overlords in the area. However; they were not know to the public as Overlords but Dan knew who they were.

All of the assassinations were being blamed on the terrorist that had been chaise out of most of the Texas cities. Allah's Right Hand still controlled most of the gangs in Texas like The Texas Syndicate and The Mexican Mafia but they only controlled parts of a few cities like Austin, Dallas, Fort Worth, and Houston. The Texas National Guard and regular Army from Fort Hood were taking care of them. Still Dan felt that a threat was still out there. Someone out there still wanted Mary Ann and her mother not to mention him and his wife and child. It was just a gut feeling but he still knew.

The next day Dan talked to all of the members of God's Soldiers. He then called them God's Angels as they would now work to protect the Compound and all that lived there.

Dan called his security company Briks' Security Agency. Those employed in his security agency were highly trained to mostly work as body guards for those that could afford it. Some of the less trained ones worked at chemical plants as gate guards. From there his security agency worked for any person that needed security and were willing to pay for their training. Before long Dan finally started getting some money coming into his businesses.

Loosing the election for County Judge was something that Dan did not see coming. The people in the town had not been hurt by the gangs and terrorist enough and reelected Judge Moore and his "do nothing" tactics. He had not kept them safe but they did not like Dan's "heavy hand" attitude. Time and time again Moore's Liberal Communist ideas did not work but he continued using the same tactics over and over again. He could not understand that when talking no longer worked you do not keep talking; you fight back. But he and the mayors of the towns in his county continued with their liberal agendas only to get overrun by the terrorist. Isn't that the definition of retarded?

Of course this did not help McNeil who had been elected as County Sheriff. Without Dan being the County Judge he stood alone in the fight against the terrorist and gangs that worked under them. Luckily for him the gangs and terrorist did not venture into their county much. Only once in a while did two or three from a gang come into their county to rob a store of it's money and food.

On one of these days Dan and Sandy took Evie and Mary Ann into town. They had two of God's Angels with them. It was the first time in almost a year that Evie and Mary Ann had been out of the Compound.

They were all in the local grocery store buying things that the Compound needed. It was more of a trip to get a few things that the women wanted. Dan noticed a van that had backed up close to the front door of the store. He did not think much about it until two pickup trucks pulled up in front of the van and masked men jumped out. When the eight men and three women ran into the store they all fired a few shots into the ceiling. Dan and the two members of Gods Angels were already waiting for them.

As Sandy took Evie and Mary Ann to the back of the store Dan and the two members of God's Angels opened fire. Instantly God's Angels took down two of the women and three of the men. Dan could hear two or three of them running towards him. Dan turned the corner and found two other customers running towards him. They came to a quick stop but Dan flagged them on towards the back where his wife was.

Dan heard a shot to his left and saw one of the men that ran in with a gun. He stepped out and fired but only wounded the man. As the man ducked behind a stack of cases of tomato soup Dan fired three more shots. Then a shot rang out to Dan's right and he fell to the floor. Unable to move he passed out.

Minutes later four of the gang members brought Sandy and the others out of the back. As they walked to the front of the store Mary Ann saw her Uncle Dan laying motionless on the floor.

"Uncle Dan." Mary Ann yelled as she ran to her uncle's side.

"Get back here you dirty brat." the remaining woman in the gang said.

The woman grabbed Mary Ann's arm and jerked her up but, when Mary Ann stood she was no longer a little girl. Instantly the Neanderthal Girl jumped on the woman ripping the woman's throat out with her teeth. Kneeling over the woman that was

160

bleeding to death the Neanderthal Girl looked around. Seeing her mother she stood and started walking towards the other three that were with her mother.

The three men started firing at the Neanderthal Girl but their bullets ricocheted off of an invisible shield around her. By time their guns were empty the Neanderthal Girl was on them. They had not planned on meeting this horror that they thought was just a joke. What they thought was just a joke killed the three of them within seconds.

Evie lead the others back to the back of the store where it was at least safer. From the back they all heard screams coming from the front of the store. Evie worried about her daughter but knew that as the Neanderthal girl she would be okay. The sounds of shattering glass and overturned racks of canned food filled the air. From time to time gunfire was heard and then suddenly it all ended with a gunshot and then the scream of one man.

Sandy left the others to checkout the front of the store. Then she saw her husband laying on the floor with Mary Ann kneeling beside him. She ran to Dan's side. He was still alive but a bullet had grazed his head. Another bullet went into his chest and did not exit.

By time the police got to the store everything was over. Two men and one woman of the gang were still alive and were taken to the hospital with police guarding them. Dan was the only other person hurt by the gunfire and was also taken to the hospital.

After getting to the hospital Dan was taken to the operating room where the bullet was removed from his chest. The bullet that everyone thought had grazed his head actually entered his skull. The .22 caliber bullet rested between his brain and skull. It was also removed but Dan was in a coma. He was sent to a private room.

The next day Davis took Evie and Mary Ann to see Dan. As they walked into the room they found Sandy sitting in a chair beside Dan's bed. She was asleep and holding her husband's hand. Evie woke her up with a gentle shake.

"Good morning sleepy head." Evie told Sandy. "How's he

doing?"

"Still in a coma." Sandy said as she cried.

"We just walked by some cops down the hall." Evie said. "They are guarding the three gang members."

"Davis." a voice came from the bed behind everyone. "Davis."

"Yes Sir." Davis quickly answered.

"The three down the hall ..." Dan said. "Are they the ones that attacked the store?"

"Yes Sir ... they are."

"Kill'em." Dan ordered.

"McNeil has three of his cops watching over them." Davis advised.

Dan thought for a moment and then said; "Get three of the Angels up here." Dan ordered Davis.

As Davis called the Compound Dan called McNeil and asked him to come see him. Knowing that Dan was in some kind of a hurry he got to the hospital as quickly as he could. The first thing he did was check on the three cops he had guarding the three gang members. Then he went down to Dan's room.

By time McNeil walked into Dan's room the three Angels were already there. Pushing his way past them he stood beside Dan's bed.

"How are you doing my friend?" McNeil asked.

"Well my friend ..." Dan started off with a big smile. "I need those three men down the hall dead for shooting me."

"Now you know I can't do that." McNeil said. "They are already looking for a reason to get rid of me so that they can replace me with a liberal communist like themselves."

"If I can get in and assassinate these three it will send a message to the others to stay away from this area ... maybe this county."

McNeil thought for a moment. "Did you say that I could use these three men of yours as deputies ... to guard those men down the hall?"

"Not that I know of." Dan did not get what McNeil was

162

suggesting.

"Wait a minute." McNeil said as he left the room.

A few minutes later McNeil returned. Then he turned his attention to the three member of God's Angels.

"You three need to go to the room that holds the three gang members." McNeil explained to them. "I sent two of the officers back to the office. The man that is still there is expecting one of you to knock him out. Then you can kill those three." Then McNeil smiled and added; "   Try not to really hurt my officer. He's helping you."

The three members of God's Angels had silencers on their pistols. They came there to do a job as quietly as possible. McNeil asked Dan to not send the three until he was gone. Five minutes after McNeil left Dan's room Dan sent his three off to do their job.

When McNeil left he walked by the room with the three gang members and waved at his officer in the room. This signaled the officer that the three members of God's Angels would be in there soon. Minutes later the three men left Dan's room.

As soon as the three members of God's Angels entered one of them hit the officer in the back of the head. Then the three shot the three gang members in the head killing all three of them. As Dan's men started to leave the room one of them saw the officer rubbing the back of his head. He stopped and asked the officer if he was awake.

"No." the officer said. "Did you have to hit me that hard?"

"Sorry man but ... I had to leave a knot to show that you were knocked out."

"I know." the officer said as he lay back down. "You guys get out's here before a nurse makes her rounds."

About fifteen minutes after the three left the room a nurse screamed. She walked into the room finding the three gang members dead. She also thought that the officer was dead until he rolled over. His story was that he was rushed by two gang members which knocked him out. They must have killed their friends for some reason.

McNeil investigated the assassination of the three gang members and in his report he also mentioned that two gang members must have killed the other three for some reason.

Dan was released from the hospital four days after the assassination of the three gang members. He was sitting at the kitchen table talking with his wife and Evie when Mary Ann walked in.

What'cha up to little one?" Dan asked Mary Ann.

"She's still out there." Mary Ann said sounding sad.

"Who is out there?" Dan asked.

"Beth … her name is Bethany … I think."

"Who is this Beth?" Dan asked Mary Ann. As Mary Ann cried she said; "She's the last Overlord and she's coming to get me."

Because of the bullet that was removed from Dan's head he was left passing out spells from time to time. However this did not stop him from trying to locate this last Overlord. Mary Ann's words continued to haunt him.

"She is the last Overlord and she is coming to get me."

Other Publications of

Vernon Gillen

Below is a list of my other novels and books that have been published.

Novels

1. "Texas Under Siege 1."
   Tale of a Survival Group Leader.
   After a man is voted as the leader of his survival group in Texas a self proclaimed Marxist president asked the United Nations troops to come in and settle down the civil unrest. The civil unrest was really nothing but Americans that complained about how he ran the country.

2. "Texas Under Siege 2."
   The Coming Storms.
   The young group leader continues to fight when the countries that made up the United Nations troops in the United States decided to take over parts of the country for their own country's to control.

3. "Texas Under Siege 3."
   The Necro Mortises Virus.
   As the group leader continues to fight the UN he learns that an old organization really controlled everything. They were known as the Bilderbergs. Tired of the resistance in Texas they release the Necro Mortises virus also known as the zombie virus.

4. "Texas Under Siege 4."
   250 Years Later.
   This novel jumps 250 years into the future where the Bilderbergs are still living with modern technology while the

other people have been reduced to living like the American Indians of the early 1800's. One of these young man stands up and fights the Bilderbergs with simple spears and arrows.

5. The Mountain Ghost 2."
    The Legend Continues.
    The Mountain Ghost continues to fight the Chinese and North Koreans soldiers that have invaded the entire southern half of the United States.

6. "The Mountain Ghost 4."
    The Ghost Warriors.
    After Russ and June have twin girls they grow up and move back south to fight the Chinese and North Koreans as the Ghost Twins. Before long they grow in numbers and call themselves the Ghost Warriors.

7. "Neanderthal."
    As a child he was injected with alien DNA. While in the Navy he was injected with Neanderthal DNA. Now because of these two injection without his knowing young Michael Gibbins changes into a six and a half foot tall Neanderthal from time to time. He grew up being bullied in school and wished that he could change into a monster so he could get back at them. Now he wishes he could take that wish back.

8. " Neanderthal. 2"
    Little Mary Ann, the daughter of Michael and Evie grows to the age of thirteen. As she grows she learns that he has many of the same abilities that her father had; and more. The problem is that she has a hard time controlling them and her anger. This causes problems for everyone watching over and trying to hide her.

Other Books

1. "Carnivores of Modern Day Texas."
A study of the animals in Texas that will not only kill you but in most cases will eat you.

2. "Zombies; According to Bubba"
After studying the Necro Mortises virus for my novel *Texas Under Siege 3*, I realized that I had a great deal of information on it. After finishing the novel I wrote this book leaving the reader to make their own decision.

Unpublished

A great deal goes into publishing a novel or book that takes time. After I write a novel I have someone proofread it. Then I have to find an artist to draw the cover picture which is hard to do. Actually finding an artist is easy but finding one that I can afford is not so easy. Then the novel or book has to be approved by the publishing company. Only then is it published. Then you have kindle and that opens another can of worms.

The fallowing novels are unpublished as I write this but will be published soon. Keep checking Amazom.com for any new novels that I have published.

1. "The Mountain Ghost 1."
The Legend of Russell Blake.
After the Chinese and North Koreans attack the southern United States two young brothers, Brandon and Russell Blake go after the invading enemy. After Brandon is killed Russell smears a white past allover his exposed skin and earns the name Mountain Ghost.

3. "The Mountain Ghost 3."
The Ghost Soldiers.

After the death of Russell Black his son, Russ, continues as to bring death and destruction to the enemy as the new Mountain Ghost.

5. "The Glassy War."

Three thousand years in the future and three galaxies away the United Planet Counsel fight and enemy that is trying to control every galaxy they come to. After both star ships crash into the planet the survivors continue to fight.

6. "The Fire Dancers."

I stopped writing this novel to start writing the Mountain Ghost series but I will be getting back to it.

I hope that you have enjoyed this novel. Please help me by sending your comments on what you thought about this novel or book by e-mailing me at <u>bubbasbooks@msn.com</u> . By doing this you will help me to be a better writer. You will also let me know what you, the public, is looking for in these types of novels and books. I have a very creative mind, a bit warped some say but, still creative but, I still need to know what you are looking for. I thank you for your assistance in this.

Vernon Gillen

Made in the USA
Columbia, SC
16 November 2022

71047667R00093